Dear [illegible]

To say [illegible] is an understatement. Serving the people of Ohio, being able to protect and help them, is my greatest thrill. Ohio, for me, offers everything I've ever wanted: horseback riding, fishing, lots of trees and plenty of lakes and rivers. It also brought me together with Leah.

Leah Stevenson is the love of my life. Until I met her, I didn't feel much like living—just surviving. I'd lost my first wife three years earlier, and the will to live sort of got sucked out of me. Firefighting became more than a way of life for me—until Leah stepped into my life that day at the Baybridge Fire Department.

Leah embodies Ohio: kind of reserved and humble, yet filled with a rich sense of self that doesn't need to be flaunted or bragged about. Ohio and Leah are about a quiet sense of integrity and timeless values that have not broken down with time. It's not hard to love them both.

Gil Gerard

LINDSAY McKENNA

A homeopathic educator, Lindsay teaches at the Desert Institute of Classical Homeopathy in Phoenix, Arizona. When she isn't teaching alternative medicine, she is writing books about love. She feels love is the single greatest healer in the world, and hopes that her books touch her readers' hearts.

Look for Lindsay McKenna's upcoming books—UNFORGIVEN, available October 2006 from Silhouette Nocturne, and BEYOND THE LIMIT, available December 2006 from HQN Books.

MEN MADE in AMERICA

Lindsay McKenna

Too Near the Fire

Silhouette® Books

Published by Silhouette Books

America's Publisher of Contemporary Romance

SILHOUETTE BOOKS®

ISBN-13: 978-0-373-36038-3
ISBN-10: 0-373-36038-X

TOO NEAR THE FIRE

Published Silhouette Books 1984, 1993

This edition published by arrangement with Harlequin Books S.A.

Visit Silhouette Books at www.eHarlequin.com

Printed in U.S.A.

Dedicated to:

Lt. Gary "Apache" Amato, who taught me the ropes of firefighting and Firefighter Paul La Neve, who saved my life at a structure fire and The firefighters of West Point Volunteer Fire Department, who opened a new chapter in my life and To all the courageous paid and volunteer women firefighters who battle not only blazes but for their right to save lives equally as well as their male counterparts

One

The sunlight was brilliant, making Leah squint as she walked out of the shade and around the corner of the two-story redbrick firehouse. The weather was typical of mid-June in Ohio: the humidity matched the high temperature. Her shoulder-length hair was drawn back severely from her oval face. Leah had learned from experience to knot her dark, walnut-colored hair into a chignon at the nape of her neck to keep it from interfering with her fire fighting duties. She slowed in front of the huge garagelike doors that housed the fire engines within the bay, her gaze lingering on the lime-colored trucks. They were all Darley engines, and she recalled with some relief that as a student at the Ohio Fire Academy, she had learned pump procedures on them. Well, at least she was familiar with the equipment—that was one thing in her favor.

Stepping into the office, Leah met a dispatcher who was attired in a light blue, short-sleeved shirt and navy gabardine slacks. Her heart dropped when she saw him scowl. She put on a smile and said, "My name is Leah Stevenson. I'm reporting for work. Is Chief Anders in?"

"Yeah, just a minute," he growled, and paged the chief. He slowly looked her up and down and Leah silently endured his scornful appraisal. Groaning inwardly, she shoved all her fears, anxieties, and questions to the back of her mind. Right now she had to try to walk a tightrope with Chief Anders. He had opposed her even more strongly than the city administrators who had fought her being hired as a member of the fire department.

Anders came in the other door, his leathery face devoid of any expression. "Stevenson?"

"Yes, sir."

"Come with me."

Leah swallowed against the lump forming in her throat and followed him through the quiet bay. She looked off to the left as they walked by a small kitchen. Three firemen looked up with curiosity as she and the chief passed by the door. The shuffle of feet and the scraping of chairs could be heard seconds after their passing. Leah could picture all three of them craning out the door to get their first look at the "lady" fire fighter. Adrenaline surged through her, adding to her shaky feeling.

Anders motioned her into his small, cluttered office. The chief was in his late fifties, a tall spare man who looked more like he belonged behind the wheel of a tractor in some cornfield than here, Leah thought. He was thin and the nervous energy that flowed through him set her on edge as he began to pace behind his dilapidated oak desk.

"Sit down," he ordered.

Leah sat on the edge of the chair, her back

ramrod straight, and carefully placed her purse on her lap. Her heart was hammering as if she were laboring up an eight-foot aerial ladder with an air pak strapped on her back. This was the real war. The ordeal of completing the basic two-hundred-hour fire fighting course at the academy would be child's play compared to the psychological battle that lay before her now. Her thoughts were interrupted by Anders.

"You got your way, Ms. Stevenson," he growled, stopping to glare across the room at her. "The mayor says I either take you into the department or our city loses its federal funding. I've been a fireman for thirty years and I ain't ever seen a female fire fighter. No woman can do this job. I don't give a damn how great your grades were at the academy or how many of your instructors swear by your abilities."

"All I ask is that you let me have a chance, Chief."

"All you're asking me to do is risk the life of one or more of my men so that you can prove me right," he hurled back.

Her throat ached with tears but she refused to allow her emotions to overwhelm her.

"Chief, I'll be the first to quit if I ever put anyone's life on the line. That's a promise."

Anders stood there regarding her silently for a long, tense minute. "It only takes once, you know. What if you're in a structure that's on fire and your partner's air pak suddenly quits functioning and he can't get oxygen? What are you gonna do? Go screaming for help like some dizzy broad?"

"No," Leah replied with a great deal more calm than she felt. "We would buddy breathe off my tank and get out of the building as quickly as possible, Chief."

"Sounds great on paper," he snorted, folding his hands and resuming his pacing. "But saying it and doin' it is two different things, Stevenson."

Leah managed a small breath of relief. Good, at least he had dropped the *Ms.* Most chiefs called their fire fighters by the last name. Instead of being offended, she was relieved. She was thankful for her six years of experience in the air force as an air controller: she was used to discipline and to being called by her last name rather than her first.

"I can keep calm in dangerous situations, Chief. I didn't work in a control tower because I was a dizzy broad. I'm used to keeping my head despite difficult circumstances," she argued coolly.

"I guess we're going to find that out, aren't we?" he railed. "Well, come with me. I'll show you where you'll be staying for the next twenty-four-hour period. You get one day on and two days off on the summer schedule. And remember, it's coed. I don't have to build you a separate bathroom or shower, Stevenson. You want to enter a man's world and our job, then you're gonna use the same facilities we do. Understand?"

Leah picked up her purse. "Yes, sir."

Anders showed her the upstairs portion of the firehouse, which was fitted with army-type bunks. The sleeping quarters had stairs as well as the standard fire pole to slide down. At the other end were lockers where civilian clothes could be stowed while the fire fighters were on duty. The chief halted in the middle of the highly polished oak floor.

"You get into uniform and then come down

to the office when you're done,'' he ordered. He dug in his pocket, thrust a badge into her hand, and then stalked off.

''Yes, sir.'' After a quick look around, Leah was relieved to find that all the on-duty firemen were downstairs in the kitchen. The only room that offered a measure of privacy was the bathroom. It was a small area housing two shower stalls, a sink with a cracked mirror above it, and a urinal. Leah slipped into her light blue shirt and navy blue slacks and pinned on the silver badge that Anders had given her. Her fingers lingered over it and she felt warm with pride.

Only officers wore gold badges; the rest of the fire fighters wore the silver ones, indicating their lesser rank. Leah smiled to herself: a silver badge distinguished her as part of the hard-working crew. She would be hauling hoses and ladders, scaling roofs with a hose and fire ax or whatever else was deemed necessary. Normally, the officer directed the fire fighting with his portable radio, but didn't get personally involved. Nonetheless, she didn't minimize the officer's duties. In the end, her life was in his hands. If the officer was a poor one, he could get her killed by ordering her into a situation that was dangerous or unstable. No, a good officer was someone she would go to hell and back for, and she wondered if they had anyone here of the caliber of the instructors down at the Ohio Fire Academy. After hanging her clothes in the only available locker, she shut it and went downstairs.

Leah stopped at the gleaming red door of the chief's office and knocked politely.

"Enter," Anders growled through it.

She opened it, almost bumping into another fireman, who was standing just inside the entrance. Fragmented impressions hit her senses. He was an officer—she could tell that by the gold badge displayed above the left breast pocket of his shirt. She was aware of height and broad shoulders. It struck Leah that he looked as if he could easily carry the weight of the world around on them if he chose. She noted the intensity of his blue eyes as he quickly perused her upturned face. Leah somehow got through and closed the door, stepping away from the officer, who remained to her left.

"Stevenson, this is Lieutenant Gil Gerard. You're being assigned to his crew."

Leah's mouth went dry as she turned, her hand extended. ''Lieutenant, a pleasure to meet you.''

The officer inclined his head and clasped her hand. ''Same here,'' he intoned, his voice low and somewhat husky.

Leah's arm tingled pleasurably. She was aware of the controlled strength of his grasp, of the rough texture of his fingers and the calluses on his palm. She forced a brief, businesslike smile to her lips and broke contact.

''Gil, take her around and show her the ropes,'' Anders said, scowling heavily. ''And remember what I told you...''

Gil pursed his mouth and opened the door, motioning her out. ''Right, Chief.''

Leah glanced up, waiting for him to close it again. She was impressed with his height and excellent physical condition. She guessed that, like herself, he worked out with weights or jogged to stay fit. That discovery made her feel an immediate camaraderie with him. It was something she shared in common with someone here at the firehouse. Lifting her chin, Leah realized he was standing quietly beside her, watching her with veiled curiosity. She met his dark blue eyes and felt heat rising from her throat into her face.

"What do you like to be called?" he asked, walking slowly down the narrow hallway.

She wanted to be flip and answer: I've been called just about everything, but you can call me Leah if you want. She fought the urge. She didn't dare allow humor into this tense situation. Above all else, she wanted to be accepted by the fire fighters. She couldn't afford to hurt anyone's feelings at this point. She had learned through harsh experience to be a shadow—seen but not heard. Otherwise the men reacted strongly and negatively to her presence. It was part of the price she paid for deciding to become a woman fire fighter.

"Most people call me Leah. My nickname down at the academy was Cat."

He tossed a glance over his shoulder. "Is that because you have pretty green eyes?" he asked, a slight smile hovering around his mouth.

Confused, Leah suppressed her own smile. Why was he treating her so nicely? Anders had made it clear that no one welcomed her here—

why should Gil Gerard be different. The officer appeared to be in his early thirties, a confident man with an open, readable face. She liked his features: He had black hair, intelligent eyes, a strong nose, and a rock-solid jaw. More than anything, Leah found herself liking his mouth. It wasn't thin or thick but mobile, expressive, with the corners lifting, indicating that he smiled a great deal. She gave a sigh and her shoulders dropped slightly. In her heart she knew that the officer she was assigned to would either make her or break her.

Meeting Gil's interested gaze, she realized she still owed him an answer to his question. "I got tagged with that down at the academy because on night exercises I could see hot spots before anyone else. They said I had eyes like a cat, so it stuck. I'd rather be called Leah, though."

Gil nodded, pursing his mouth. He halted at the bay, putting his hands on his lean hips. "It pays to have good night vision," he agreed amicably. "Come on, I'll introduce you to our ladies here in the bay and then show you where we spend most of our time when we aren't polishing the engines or the floors."

He missed nothing in proudly showing her the "ladies." Most fire fighters referred to the trucks as female. The self-contained breathing apparatus, or MSA air paks, were resting on specially constructed steel braces behind the drivers' seats. When the alarm went off, whoever was assigned to get into air paks would leap into the "jump seats," slip the gear over their shoulders, belt up, and donning air masks, ready to enter a burning building by the time they arrived on the scene. The air pak enabled a fire fighter to work in a smoke-filled structure without being overcome by the noxious atmosphere or deadly fumes.

Leah caressed the shiny lime fender of one Darley engine with her long, slender fingers as Gil stopped near the front of it. He patted the truck affectionately. "You'll soon find out we have names for all these gals."

"And a few curse words, I'll bet," she added, smiling hesitantly. There was something about Gil that made her feel safe about letting down her guard and allowing a little bit of her private self to show.

"Well, we have Lady here, and naturally, she

is one. She behaves real well no matter what the weather conditions are or how sticky a situation gets at a fire scene.'' He walked over to the second pumper. ''This one we call the Beast because she always gives her driver a problem. A real cold starter. Won't cooperate with you at all if she's throwing one of her fits.'' He grinned, his teeth white and even against his darkly bronzed skin. ''Just like some women.''

Leah shrugged. ''Maybe she just needs a more gentle touch...a little more understanding,'' she said hesitantly.

One eyebrow rose in response. ''Could be. Did you have much experience driving these rigs down at the academy?''

''Yes, as a matter of fact they had Darleys.''

He nodded. ''Good. I'll keep that in mind. We may need you there if we find ourselves in a bind,'' he murmured, sounding pleased.

She frowned. At a paid fire station each fire fighter was assigned a specific job and rarely stepped into any other specialty. If a man was a driver and pump operator on an engine, he always remained in that position. It sounded as though she would be a ''gopher,'' doing the myriad jobs that were demanded of a fire fighter at a scene, but having no one specialty. Though she didn't feel comfortable with Gil's comment, she said nothing as she followed him back to the next pumper.

"This is Molly, our aerial ladder. We've got some three- to five-story buildings around here and occasionally we need her services. The last one here is Lizzy and she's our squad truck. We take her out on extrication runs, medical emergencies, and other miscellaneous duties." Gil halted, resting his tall frame against the squad truck, and looked at her for a long moment.

"I understand that you specialized in auto extrication down at the academy."

"Yes, I loved it. I joined a volunteer fire department while I was down at Reynoldsburg and the extrication officer, Harry Billings, sort of took me under his wing and showed me the ropes."

Gil looked impressed. "Harry's one of the best," he agreed, his voice taking on a new tone of respect. "I did all my training under him down at the academy years ago. Did you make any runs?"

"Five," she admitted, deliberately trying not to recall those scenes. She hadn't been ready for the blood, the screams of the people trapped inside the wrecked cars. No one had prepared her for the emotional side of the work. She had been sick more than once after the victims had been extricated and were on their way to a hospital in an ambulance. Harry had stoically waited until she was done and then they collected the gear. His only words were: "You'll get used to it after a while, Leah." And her returning comment had been: "I doubt it."

"Blood bother you?" Gil asked, interrupting her thoughts.

How should she answer? If she was honest, it did. But if she owned up to it, he would think her weak and incapable. "No," she lied.

He reacted as if he'd expected no other answer. "Depending on how you work out here, Leah, I need someone besides myself who can run the extrication equipment. I get called in every time we have that sort of job." He smiled, and his face lost its momentary seriousness. "I have other things to do during my days off, so maybe we can eventually work out some sort of a system."

"You get that many calls?" she asked, a little surprised.

Gil nodded. "Yeah, we're right off a turnpike and a major interstate. And because northeast Ohio is so heavily industrialized, we have more spills of hazardous materials here than in any other part of the state."

Now it was her turn to raise her eyebrows. "How many fire calls do you get a year?"

"About three hundred fire runs and two hundred miscellaneous ones, including mutual aid with four other volunteer departments that surround our town's border. We keep pretty busy. You like to fight fires?"

She considered it a silly question. "Of course," she answered, stung. "I didn't put myself through the academy for a lark."

Gil held up both hands. "Easy, I was only wondering."

She felt a rapport with him and decided to take a chance. "Lieutenant, why aren't you treating me like the plague? Most fire fighters would."

He looked at her thoughtfully for a moment, shifting his weight to one leg. "A couple of reasons, I guess. One, I'm not from Baybridge originally. Two, I'd like to consider myself open-minded about a woman doing this job.'' He frowned. ''If you prove to be able to handle the runs, I'll be a hundred and ten percent behind you. But if you don't cut it, I'll be the first to recommend your dismissal,'' he warned.

She compressed her lips. He was like all the rest. She would have to be twice as good as any male rookie and make half as many mistakes as any other man who might hold the same job. Well, it was too late to turn back and slink into her old way of life. When she had divorced Jack she had said goodbye to the suffocating lifestyle that she had led for six years.

''Are you saying that the rest of the fire fighters are locals?''

He ran his strong-looking fingers through his hair, pushing a stray strand off his forehead. ''They are. As two outsiders, we might even call them clannish and backward,'' he admitted ruefully. ''This town is an agricultural area for the most part, with a few coal mines and coal trucks thrown in.''

Leah stepped away from him. She was drawn

too easily to his quiet magnetism. He was handsome in an interesting way, a way that attracted her and at the same time frightened her. "Why are you being so helpful?" she demanded.

"Until you give me cause to treat you differently, I won't discriminate on the basis of your sex."

She eyed him distrustfully. She had run into two types of fire fighter thus far. One type disdained her completely and treated her with angry silence. The other type tried to seduce her, seemingly turned on by the thought of a woman doing a dangerous job. Gil Gerard seemed to be the latter...but she wasn't sure.

She touched her brow, managing a fleeting smile of apology. "I'm sorry. I'm sure I sound like I've got a chip on my shoulder. It's just that I've endured a hell of a lot of chauvinism."

"Yeah, you got a little chip on your shoulder," he commented, a slow grin pulling at his mouth. His eyes were dark and sparkled with mirth. "And I do have to admit, I did fight fires with a woman before I joined here, so I have a little more experience in the matter than the rest of the fellas."

Leah's eyes widened. "You did?"

Gil shrugged. "I was a volunteer fireman before I joined a paid department."

"For how long?"

"Five years."

"And how long have you been paid?"

"Three."

She stared at him. "And you've made officer already?" There was a newfound respect in her voice. Being a fire officer wasn't some cushy job gotten through political pull. No, the man or woman selected had to have a lot of intelligence and experience to be sending a fire team into unknown and many times dangerous situations.

"I'm good at taking tests," he said, trying to minimize his credentials, as he led her around to the opposite wall where the turn-out gear was neatly hung.

"You have to be more than a good test taker to get the rank," she observed seriously, stopping at his shoulder.

"Hmm, I suppose. Let's try and find some gear that will fit you." He emphasized the word *fit*. For the next half hour Leah tried on every coat and every pair of boots and bunker pants in the station. Nothing fit. It was all too large. Especially the boots. She sat on the chair, sliding off the last pair.

"We'll have to order you an outfit," Gil acknowledged as he hung the last coat back up on its hook. "Probably take a couple of weeks, if I know our dispatcher."

Leah looked up at him sharply. "I'm not about to sit out fire calls for that period of time!"

"I wouldn't let you anyway. For now, let's get the closest fit, and tomorrow when we're off duty I'll take you up to Cleveland and we'll get you some decent gear. Deal?"

Either he was an angel or he had an angle, Leah decided, mulling over the tempting invitation. She had just rented an apartment and most of her articles were still packed. It wouldn't be much fun spending the day there alone. Furthermore, she was unacquainted with the area and knew it would be better if he were along. Still...she didn't want to socialize with anyone here at the station. She had read enough articles in *Fire Chief Magazine* by women fire fighters to realize that irate wives would probably be calling to see if their husbands were "safe" from the new female at the station. Idly, she looked at his left hand. There was no wedding band there. That didn't mean anything, though, and Gil had mentioned that he did like his days off. Many times the stress of fire fighting drove a wedge into a family, and divorce was too often the result.

"Well?"

"Oh...sorry, I was thinking. I'd appreciate it, Lieutenant, but I don't want to take you away from—"

"No problem," he returned smoothly. "I've made it a point to make sure my team has the best protection and the most training possible, and you'll be no exception to that rule. You can't effectively do your job in a pair of poorly fitting boots. You'd be falling all over yourself."

Leah grinned. "That brings back a lot of memories. For the first two weeks at the academy I had a coat that was four sizes too big and boots that came off my feet every time I took a step."

''You must have been damn good, then,'' he praised, ''because I got a chance to look at your academy records. Lousy-fitting gear would be enough to put some fire fighters out of commission altogether.''

She put her sensible black shoes back on and then stood up. ''I couldn't let that happen to me. I just gritted my teeth and told myself I was going to do it better than any of them, and I guess I did.''

He tilted his head, studying her in a new light. ''I like your aggressiveness, Leah. Come on, let me introduce you to the rest of the crew. It's almost time to pick straws to see who makes dinner tonight.'' The other three fire fighters looked up when Gil escorted her into the kitchen-and-dining area. Leah automatically tensed, sensing the coldness in the air.

''Fellas, this is Leah Stevenson, our new member. She's got eyes like a cat, from what she tells me.'' He pointed to a small wiry man who had dark hair and eyes and an olive complexion. ''This is Tony DiGeronimo, but everyone calls him Apache even though he's Italian because no one can pronounce his last name in a hurry. He's been on board for seven years and is one hell of a fire fighter.''

Tony sized her up. ''Welcome aboard,'' he said, smiling openly.

''And this good-looking string bean is Sam Wilson. He's our driver and pump operator. He's been on board for fifteen years and there isn't a thing he doesn't know about Darley pumps.''

Sam managed a sour grin, nervously turning his coffee mug in his hands, his lanky arms on the table. ''Except for the Beast out there.''

She smiled shyly, trying desperately to appear relaxed beneath the men's intense scrutiny. ''Hi, Sam.''

Gil motioned to his right toward a man who was scowling darkly at her. ''This is Duke Saxon and he's been with us for three years. I think he's been involved in about every dangerous structure fire we've ever made a run on. Always been at the wrong place at the right time.''

Duke stared in her direction; his black eyes were vicious looking. He was a huge, heavily muscled man, and it was clear he resented her presence.

Gil pulled out a chair for her. "Have a seat, Leah. How about some coffee?"

She turned. "That would be great. Thanks."

"Since when did you ever wait on any of us?" Duke growled.

The rest of the fire fighters laughed nervously as Gil walked nonchalantly to the draining board and pulled down a cup. "If you were as good-looking, Duke, I might have done the same for you," Gil retorted, his smile fixed. There was an unspoken warning in his look.

Leah sensed an immediate antagonism between the two men. Great, she thought, that's all I need, to walk into the middle of a sparring session between an officer and a fire fighter. She thanked Gil nervously as he placed the cup in front of her, then took a quick sip and burned her tongue.

"Okay, who's cooking today?" Gil asked, leaning against the draining board.

Duke snorted. "Let her."

She raised her head, meeting his black glare. "I wasn't hired as chief cook and bottle washer, Duke. I'll take my turn like everyone else."

The silence froze around them like brittle ice. Leah heard Gil sigh as he came over to the table. There was a deck of cards on the table and he picked them up, spreading them into a fan-like position. "Okay, everyone pick a card. Low man—that is, person—will be cook and bottle washer for the shift."

To Leah's relief, Apache got the two of hearts and he growled, getting to his feet.

"Okay, guys, you're gettin' spaghetti and meatballs—again," he warned.

Sam Wilson groaned. "Give me the Rolaids now...."

The fire fighters kept up their banter all evening, excluding her unless Gil made a concerted effort to include her in the conversation. Leah sat in one of the old frayed chairs and watched television with the rest of them, but she wasn't really listening to it. Her heart was filled with pain at the undercurrent of bitterness the men felt toward her. Duke made no bones about it at all and Sam ignored her as if she didn't exist.

Wanting something to do, Leah got up and went out into the semilighted bay, walking around each engine to begin familiarizing herself with the equipment and where it was stowed. Each compartment held some particular instrument that might be needed on a moment's notice at the scene of a fire. In one, all the electrical cords, a fan, and extra outlets were stored. In the rear of the main pumper were several spare air bottles. During a hot blaze, a fire fighter could go through two or three cylinders; each tank only contained thirty minutes' worth of air supply, and fighting fire made a person breathe deeply and heavily because of the physical exertion.

She had spent more than a half hour out in the bay alone when she heard someone walking up behind her. Turning, she saw it was Duke Saxon.

"Whatya doing, trying to impress the lieutenant by being gung ho?" he sneered.

Leah moistened her lips and ordered her body to remain relaxed although her heart was hammering wildly in her chest. She lifted her chin and met his hooded stare.

"I don't have to impress anyone."

"Yeah, you do."

"Look, it's pretty obvious you don't want

me around here, and I can live with that,'' she began tightly.

''Bet you had to live with that down at the academy, too. You may be a good-lookin' broad, but that don't make you no fireman, honey. Hell, if you weigh over one-forty, I'll quit the force.''

''Weight's got nothing to do with it,'' she countered icily.

''Like hell it don't. You tryin' to tell me that if I get in trouble in a burning structure and you gotta drag me out with air pak on that you can do it? I weigh close to three hundred pounds with all that gear on.'' He snorted, his eyes narrowing. ''No way, honey, no way.'' He raised his finger, pointing at her. ''But I'm gonna tell you something and it had better stick the first time around—you screw up with me and it will be your last day on the force.''

Her body was galvanized with fury. ''I'll remember that, Saxon,'' she promised, her voice barely above a whisper.

''You do that, honey. Sam and Apache feel the same. None of us wants you around here except that damn lieutenant of ours.'' Duke shook his head. "He's an outsider like you are, so what the hell does he know?"

"Stevenson?" It was Gil's voice ringing through the bay. She gasped softly, turning in his direction. Through the dimness she saw his head and broad shoulders, looking incredibly strong in the shadows. Saxon gave her one last glare and turned away, then melted back into the darkness, avoiding Gil completely.

"Listen, before you turn in tonight I want—" he stopped, frowning. "You all right?"

"Yeah, sure," she muttered.

Gil looked around and then back at her. "You look pale," he observed.

"It's nothing," she ground out. "Now what is it you want me to do?"

He handed her several manuals. "If you need some bedtime reading, here are the rules and regulations of the department. If we have to make a run tonight I'm going to hold you back and let you play gopher. I'll be working up a training schedule for you in the next week so that I can get acquainted with your weak and strong points." He appraised her closely.

"You're pretty good at hiding things, aren't you?" he asked, his voice dropping to a husky whisper.

Startled by the concern in his voice, Leah reacted more strongly than she had intended. "I don't know what you're talking about."

He leaned against the engine, one hand resting on the side of his head. "I saw Duke sneaking back to the kitchen, so I figured you had a run-in with him. He's not known for mincing his words and he holds a real macho attitude toward women in general. You know the type—keep them barefoot and pregnant."

Leah felt her body trembling with repressed anger and she found no humor in his statement. She remained silent beneath his scrutiny, feeling acutely uncomfortable.

"Look," he began heavily, "if you're having trouble with any of these guys, let me know."

She nearly laughed. "And rat on them? That's great, Lieutenant. I'm sure that will go over big. No, thanks. I learned down at the academy to take my lumps and keep my mouth shut."

Gil frowned and stood upright. "That may have worked well down there, Stevenson, but it won't here. This is a permanent job for you and you'll probably be with this crew for at least a year. I want to stop any problems before they get started. And I don't consider your coming to me as ratting. It's my job to make sure my crew works as a smooth unit not only for your sake, but for the safety of the people we rescue as well."

She moved restlessly away from him, wanting to believe him but afraid to. "I'll work it out my own way," she said, then turned and went upstairs to the bunk room.

It was nearly eleven when she closed the manual, unable to stop the words from blurring before her eyes. She sighed and sat up on the edge of her bunk. There were five beds: three on one side and two on the other. It was quiet and the silence only emphasized the loneliness Leah felt. She looked slowly around the small room, feeling terribly bereft. Going back downstairs she pulled her boots and bunker pants from beneath her coat and helmet and carried them up to the sleeping quarters. Dutifully arranging the black canvas bunker pants so that they would be accessible in case of an alarm, she shortened the red suspenders for her height. After taking a pair of cotton pajamas and her robe and toilet articles, she went into the shower room. Leah was sure that the rest of the men would wait until she was safely in bed before coming up.

By midnight she was snuggled into her bunk beneath a light sheet. She lay awake, staring into the darkness. Her first job…and no one except Lt. Gil Gerard cared if she was here or not. And he seemed to think of her as one more management problem he would have to deal with. She sighed softly, her heart aching over the idiocy of it all.

What was wrong with these thick-headed firemen? She was perfectly capable of doing the job and helping to save lives. And wasn't that what it was all about? Saving lives and property? Who the hell cared if it was a man or a woman who did the saving? Did the child she'd rescued last month care that she was a woman? And what about the old man with a heart attack to whom she had administered CPR? Or the man she'd cut out of a mangled car whose bleeding she had staunched until paramedics could arrive? Leah took a deep, unsteady breath, finally closing her eyes. Why didn't they see the motivation behind her actions? She didn't want to invade a man's world; she wanted only to be given the chance to work at something that gave her a sense of accomplishment.

Two

Leah was violently thrown awake by the fire alarm droning through the bunk room. The lights automatically came on, and she threw her legs across the bed and climbed into her bunker pants and boots. She gave no thought to how she looked in her cotton pajama top as she made a leap for the pole, slid neatly down it, and landed quickly on the first floor.

CAR ACCIDENT AT THE CORNER OF CARSON AND FORBES, a disembodied voice announced over the loudspeaker set in the bay.

She could hear the men calling to one another as she quickly shrugged into her black coat and threw the heavy visored helmet on her head. Duke Saxon whipped past her, running for his gear. She turned and was confronted by Gil. His eyes were narrowed and she could see him thinking out the situation. The squad truck was fired up and so was the Darley pumper called Lady. The officer looked directly at her.

"You ride shotgun with me in the squad. Duke, you and Apache get into air pak," he ordered calmly.

She trotted to the squad and slid into the passenger side. Before getting in to drive, Gil started up the air compressor in the rear of the squad truck. Leah automatically reprimanded herself. She should have been doing that instead of him.

The bay was filled with the sound of roaring engines, the flash of whirling red-and-white lights as they drove out into the hot, humid night. Gil pointed to the radio.

"Say 'Squad Fifty-One Signal Twelve,'" he ordered.

She nodded, picked up the mike, and repeated the message. Blinking, Leah put it back on the clip, her lips set in a thin line as the siren wailed through the empty streets of the sleeping town.

"How far away is this accident?" she asked, her voice strangely husky with adrenaline.

"Five miles."

"Any idea of how bad a wreck it is?"

"No. Dispatch said it was called in by the state police."

She nodded, automatically going over the various types of equipment that might be utilized in this kind of situation.

"When we get to the scene I want you to stand by here at the squad. I hope like hell it's a simple extrication, but you never know. Apache and Duke will pull off the inch and a half and approach the car first. If there's fire they'll knock it down, then be ready to cover us during the extrication. We don't want any sparks to start a fire and blow us all away."

Leah felt her heart pumping strongly and she pulled her heavy fire-retardant gloves on a little tighter. Like the rest of her gear, they didn't fit and she shook her head. All she needed was a pair of bumbling hands while she was trying to work at top speed.

As they drew up on a lonely farm road, Leah spotted the white state trooper car, its light flashing forlornly in the night. Gil took the mike off the hook and ordered the engine to halt before it got to the wreck. He glanced at Leah.

''Stay here,'' he ordered, then climbed out and trotted up to the scene of the accident to assess the situation.

Tightening her helmet strap against her chin until it was snug, she realized with a sinking sensation that it was a bad wreck. The entire front end of a red Buick had been smashed as it hit a utility pole. The car had come to rest in a wide, deep ditch and now looked like a folded accordion. She saw Gil raise the portable radio to his mouth and almost immediately was aware of Apache and Duke trotting forward with a charged inch and a half line. That meant fire and perhaps a gasoline spill. Her heartbeat increased. It meant twice the danger. Once positioned, Apache opened the nozzle, sending a semi-fog stream beneath the rear of the auto.

Gil returned at a steady trot and slid back into the squad. Leah glanced tensely over at him.

"What have we got?" She surprised herself. She had used the word *we.* Wasn't that what fire fighting was all about...teamwork? If he noticed her use of the word, he said nothing.

"Got a drunken teenager with his legs pinned beneath the steering wheel. He's unconscious," he muttered tightly. He threw the squad into gear and moved just close enough to string the compressor lines to the smoldering wreck. The truck was kept at a safe distance in case the car exploded. It was senseless to wreck expensive equipment.

Leah got out, shading her eyes as the pumper's quartz lights flashed on. The chatter of the portable generator in the side compartment of the engine added to the cacophony of sounds. A glare of surrealistic light enveloped the accident scene. The other two fire fighters were hosing down the rear of the mangled car, forcing the leaking gasoline away from the area and diluting it with the water. Gil handed her the chisel and a pry bar.

"That door is jammed. We've got to get it open. I'll bring the come-a-long and the other gear."

The trooper at the scene helped them, and within moments they were set up. Her heart rate was high, her knees shaky with adrenaline. The sharp odor of gas stung her nostrils. Gil came up.

"Cut through the door handle," he ordered. She was glad her visor was down as Apache and Saxon approached, spraying a fine mist of water over her. The droplets blanketed her head and shoulders as she got ready to cut. The water would reduce the chance of a stray spark starting a fire. Placing the power chisel against the metal, she started it and a reverberating sound rent the air. Leah leaned her weight into the chisel, cutting through the thinner metal of the door around the handle. She prayed that it would be possible to manipulate the inner door mechanism so that they wouldn't have to literally tear the door off its hinges.

"Leah?" Gil called.

She finished the job and quickly set aside the chisel. After kneeling down and peeling back the metal, she took a flashlight from her pocket and studied the mechanism. She was vaguely aware of Gil leaning over. Shakily she reached into the door, jerking at one of the long bars. They both heard a distinct *click* and Gil straightened up, ordering her to stand back. He gave the door one good yank and it fell open.

"Good work," he praised. "Make a hole in the front windshield so we can get the come-a-long around the steering wheel."

She struggled with her ill-fitting boots as she moved gawkily around in the darkness to the other side of the car.

"His pulse is weak," the trooper shouted, leaning in through the passenger window to help cover the driver with a wool blanket.

Leah staggered into the ditch, pitching forward, one boot having slipped halfway off her foot.

"Come on, Stevenson!" Saxon yelled, making an angry gesture with his free arm. "Hurry it up!"

Leah pushed back her helmet, which had tipped forward, and struggled to her feet, embarrassment flooding her. As she reached the other side she took the pointed end of the pry bar and made an oblong hole along the passenger side of the windshield. That done, Gil passed another wool blanket through his side of the glass to her. Leah grabbed it, getting ready to jerk it outward and away from the inert driver.

"Keep him covered," Gil told the trooper. The trooper nodded and pulled the protective blanket over the boy's head.

"Go ahead," the officer yelled, and turned his head away to protect himself from flying glass.

Gil glanced up. "Count of three, Leah."

The windshield came out cleanly with one good jerk. The glass popped outward, dancing across the hood and splintering on the ground. As swiftly as she could, Leah came around to the driver's side and helped station the come-a-long across the mangled hood of the car. The trooper stood clear while she wrapped the heavy chain around the steering column three times and rehooked it outside the windshield. She could hear the wail of an ambulance approaching as she leaned into the driver's side of the car, focusing her flashlight on the teenager. Leah heard him groan and put her gloved hand on his shoulder to steady him.

"Go ahead," she called to Gil, "start tightening it. I'll let you know when his legs are free." The boy moaned once again and Leah divided her attention between him and the steering column. The chains grew taut, creaking and straining, and the steering column slowly yielded to the five thousand pounds of pressure being applied by the come-a-long. She automatically shielded the boy with her body, wanting to protect him in case the chain or any part of the equipment snapped and flew loose. A broken chain could be deadly and she didn't want the driver injured any more than he was already.

"It's moving," she reported. "Another two inches and we'll have it."

The trooper had moved back to the passenger side, and now he crawled in carefully through the open window. "Here, I got the short backboard and a neck collar from your driver," he offered.

Sweat ran down into her eyes and she blinked them, trying to get rid of the smarting sensation. "Thanks. You just steady the kid when the rest of that pressure comes off his thighs," she directed.

"Say...you aren't—"

Leah grinned, her face glistening with perspiration. "Yeah, I'm a woman." She applied the surgical collar to keep the boy's neck stabilized in case he had sustained a spinal injury.

The trooper said nothing, expertly sliding the backboard between the driver and the seat after she had fastened the collar. Leah could feel the trickle of sweat running down her rib cage and had a wild desire to scratch it. She lowered her head, watching Gil as he bore down with all his weight against the handle of the come-a-long. In one part of her mind she thanked God he was turning out to be as good a fire officer as she had thought he would be.

Just as the last of the mangled steering column came off the boy's thighs, Leah sat up, facing the semiconscious driver. She pushed up the protective plastic visor of her helmet. The smell of gasoline and alcohol filled her senses.

The trooper flashed his light down on the boy's legs. "He's coming around," was all he said.

Leah was in the process of getting out of her kneeling position when the boy screamed, flailing his arms wildly. His hand caught her solidly in the nose and she was slammed backward, tumbling out of the car head first. Leah scrambled blindly to her knees and reached out to grab the boy's arms. Adrenaline surged through her and she shouted at the trooper to grab his right arm while she tackled the left.

"It's okay, okay," she breathed heavily against the boy's ear. With her left hand, she placed her glove against his shoulder. "You're safe, safe…you hear me…everything's going to be all right," she crooned. She had seen many teenagers who mixed alcohol with drugs. They would often become wild and hysterical upon regaining consciousness. This kid was no exception.

Leah gritted her teeth, using the leverage of her body to control his wild movements. "Lieutenant—" she yelled, seeing that the trooper had no room to maneuver properly to keep the kid down. She didn't want to hurt the boy, but at the same time, she knew he could do further damage to himself if she let him flail wildly around in the car. Gil appeared from the right, his face tense and grim.

"Okay," he ordered huskily, "we'll both hold him until the ambulance people can get up here. They're bringing the stretcher now. Apache, I smell more gas. Get back there and hose the area down again."

She was sobbing for breath as she struggled with the boy. "You're going to be fine," she said softly. "Just fine. In a few minutes we'll have you on your way to the hospital...."

Her voice finally began to have a soothing effect. He suddenly stopped wrestling and leaned back, his eyes wide and dilated. Gil sucked in a deep breath of air.

"You're okay, son. Can you hear me?"

"Ahhh, man, let me outa here! I don't need no hospital. I'm okay."

Leah tightened her grip on the boy's shoulder and looked sharply at Gil, who was inches away. He met her glance and gave her a momentary nod. So much was conveyed in that one look, it was as though for a moment they had read each other's minds. In another two minutes the boy had fainted and the paramedics were on hand to take command of the situation. Gil slid his hand beneath her arm and helped her stand.

Her knees were surprisingly shaky and she leaned against his strong body. Faintness swept over her and she called his name, her voice sounding very far away. She was aware of his arm sliding around her body. Her head lolled back against his shoulder and she closed her eyes, surrendering to the pain shooting up toward her brow.

"Leah!" he whispered, lowering her gently to the pavement. Gil anxiously searched her drawn features in the glaring light provided by the pumper. She was semi-conscious, trying to raise her hand toward her face. "No," he ordered softly, gripping her hand. Cradling her against his body, he removed the helmet from her head. His heart beat heavily in his chest as he realized how much pain she was experiencing. In that moment Gil was aware of another feeling. He admired her courage. Even now she wouldn't whimper or moan aloud. He yanked off his glove and cupped her chin, which was beginning to swell. He twisted to the left and yelled for Apache.

Apache trotted over. "What happened?" he asked, kneeling down beside Leah.

"That damn kid hit her in the face when he became conscious. You take her helmet, Apache. I'll carry her over to the cab of the pumper. Have Sam get the first-aid kit out." Worriedly he looked her over. "We may have to get her to the hospital if her nose is broken."

Apache grimaced as he quickly rose to his feet. "This is the thanks we get for saving that kid's life. Great. Just great."

Leah drew in a ragged breath as pain jabbed her temple. She was aware of Gil's body pressed against her, aware of the drumlike beat of his heart against her ear as he rested her head on his broad chest. She tried desperately to fight off the faintness, but the pain made it difficult. Gil gathered her into his arms, lifting her upward. "I wanted to hold you, but this is a hell of a way to get the chance to do it," he murmured, humor tinging his husky voice.

She had never felt so safe as in Gil's strong arms. She rested her head on his shoulder as he carried her toward the pumper. The voices of the other fire fighters drifted in and out. Eventually, Leah became aware that she was in the warmth of the cab. Gil kept one arm around her shoulders so she wouldn't fall sideways or forward, possibly injuring herself further. His breath was warm and moist against her face as he leaned over, cleaning her lips and jaw.

Leah sat perfectly still, amazed at how gentle he could be with those large, well-shaped hands. Her hair, once knotted securely, had unraveled, the dark tresses spilling across her shoulders.

''Take it easy, babe,'' Gil soothed, carefully blotting away the blood. ''Here,'' he instructed as he placed a cloth in her right hand, ''hold this against your nose. I'm going to do a little pressing on the bridge to see if you've broken it.'' He leaned closer, his eyes dark and shadowed as he surveyed her. ''You know something,'' he went on as if conversationally discussing the weather, ''you're good-looking even in turn-out gear.'' He grinned, carefully examining the bridge of her nose. ''Hurt?''

''No,'' she mumbled. The bleeding was finally beginning to lessen. Her heart pulsed strongly each time he grazed her skin. She opened her eyes, looking up into his concerned, handsome features. There was an incredible gentleness about him as he worked. It served to relax her. Her mind was still foggy and she struggled to remember the conversation he had had with her out on the road. Had he really said he wanted to hold her? Leah chided herself for the feeling of excitement that swept through her. She couldn't afford to get involved with anyone at the fire department. And especially not the man who was caring for her at this moment. Leah yearned to rest her head against his shoulder, close her eyes, and feel safe, but that was impossible.

Gil was satisfied. "Doesn't look broken," he said. "How are you feeling?"

Leah wanted to say: I feel safe in your arms. Instead, she rolled her head to the left, meeting his intense gaze. "Fine. Really, I can make it now."

A partial smile pulled at his well-shaped mouth. His blue eyes took on a bemused gleam. "Hey," he chided softly, "I'm your friend, remember? I'm not out to prove you can't make it as a fire fighter. Now, let's try this one more time. How are you feeling?"

Leah was grateful that the cab was semidark

or he would have seen her blushing. "I've got a horrible headache and my jaw feels swollen."

His grin broadened and he gave her a gentle embrace. "That's more like it. Feel like walking back to the squad with me?"

Leah's heart soared with unexplained happiness. She gave a hesitant nod. Holding the sterile gauze against her nose, Gil helped her out of the cab. The other three fire fighters gathered around, concern written on their sweaty faces. One part of her wanted to be independent of Gil. Were they thinking she was weak? She couldn't bear the thought and tried to walk under her own power. Gil placed a protective arm around her waist, forcing her to lean against him.

"You okay, Leah?" Apache asked, the first to come up.

"Yeah," she answered, "just a bad nosebleed."

The Italian fireman reached out, giving her a careful pat on her shoulder. "I was watching you during the extrication. You did a hell of a good job. If that kid had punched me in the running lights, I'd have hit him back. You did good under the circumstances."

Leah managed a weak smile. "Thanks, Apache. It means a lot to me."

"How are you holding up?" Gil asked, leaning down to inspect her face as they walked down the highway toward the squad.

"All I want to do now is get back and take a hot shower."

Gil slowed his stride to match her own. "You're going to need a steak, too. Your left eye is swollen. It ought to be black by tomorrow morning."

Leah groaned. "Just what I need."

He opened the door for her and then slid into the driver's seat. "When the local reporter comes down tomorrow morning to check on our runs, he'll see you and think we beat you up."

The ambulance had already left with the injured driver and a wrecker had arrived and was pulling the remains of the car out of the ditch.

Leah hesitantly returned his smile and shut the door. She cradled her helmet in her hands, allowing her head to rest against the rear of the cab.

Gil snapped off the beacon lights. He loosened his helmet and handed it to her. She took it without another word, staring down at the yellow color. Lieutenants always wore yellow turn-out gear and helmets; assistant chiefs wore red and the chief wore white. Gil put the truck in gear and started back toward town. Suddenly he smiled, his even white teeth stark against the sweat and grime on his face. "Just sit back and relax now. I'll take good care of you."

"You really don't have to make such a fuss over me," she protested.

"Lady, you're worth making a fuss over, believe me."

The words pleased her and Leah did as she was ordered. Watching Gil through half-closed eyes, she found it hard not to stare at him. Normally, men did not arouse her curiosity or, indeed, any sort of emotional reaction. Jack had seen to that, she thought bitterly. She took in Gil's clean profile, marveling at the strength stamped in his features. Yet he had shown her he was capable of gentleness, too. Every time she remembered his touch, her body automatically responded. It puzzled her. She barely knew the man.

Gil broke the pleasant silence after a few

minutes. He turned to glance at her in the darkness. "Hell of a note," he said wryly. "On your first run you get hit." He smiled. "Figure it out—we save a kid's life and you get punched."

A grin edged her lips; a feeling of pride swelled in her breast. "It was worth every bit of pain and embarrassment," she assured him. "A life was saved and that's all that matters to me."

He reached out, hesitantly touching her hair, running his fingers down the silken tresses. "Your life matters too, you know." His eyes became cobalt colored as he said, "Next time, Leah, don't put yourself in such a vulnerable position when you know the driver is either on drugs or alcohol. He might have hit you in the eye and blinded you." He shook his head, a mournful note in his voice. "God, you have beautiful eyes. I'd hate to see anything happen to them." He rested his hand on her shoulder and gave it a squeeze. "You just be more careful" was all he said.

Her eyes widened with disbelief. Leah couldn't tear her gaze from his. He cared. He truly cared what happened to her. To her surprise, tears filled her eyes. She quickly looked away, hoping the darkness would hide them. "I'll try," she mumbled.

"Why don't you rest," he suggested.

"No, thanks," she murmured.

"You don't have to play tough when we're by ourselves," he said, glancing over at her.

Leah gave him a startled look. "What?"

"Give in and rest. I'm not going to call you weak just because others might. You put in a good performance on short notice. You deserve the downtime."

The huskiness in his voice sent another tingle of pleasure through her tired, aching body. "You should have let me help clean up," she muttered.

"Why? You did your share of assigned duties. You don't have to be a superwoman."

She grinned tiredly. "No, but it sure helps if you're a woman in the fire service."

"Don't push yourself so hard," he coaxed huskily. "You did a good job. Matter of fact, the state trooper at the site was Sergeant Mike Ryan, and he's back there shaking his head in disbelief."

"Oh?"

"Didn't realize you were a woman until you started soothing that kid by talking to him. He said you did one hell of a job. And believe me, Ryan's a hard case to work with at an accident scene."

Her heart swelled with joy but she tried to control her reactions. "It takes more than one extrication to make you good," she returned soberly. "When I have a few more under my belt, I'll feel a lot more confident than I did out there tonight."

"If you weren't confident, it didn't show." He scratched his head. "I underestimated you."

"In what way?"

"You're a lot harder to read than I first thought. Make me a promise, Leah?"

She stared at him. "What kind?" she asked tentatively.

"You're defensive, but I guess I don't blame you. I'm not asking, but ordering you, to report to me if there's ever a time in the future when you get injured. Don't try and fake it, okay? It's necessary to work as a team, and it's important to communicate your full condition.

Don't downplay it because of your bullheadedness."

"I'm not stubborn," she flared. "I learned the hard way down at the academy that if you showed any emotion you were considered weak. And if a fireman thinks you're weak, he won't work with you or—worse—he'll try to take over." She sat back, staring moodily into the darkness. "You don't learn much if someone is always taking over, Lieutenant."

"Call me Gil. And somehow, I doubt that you let too many male rookies take over for you down there," he drawled. "Now, you want to make me that promise?"

She remained quiet for a long time, mulling it over in her aching head. If she could trust what she saw, Gil Gerard was one hundred and ten percent behind her. He actually seemed excited about her performance and that gave her a needed boost of confidence. She found herself liking him more than she should. But then, he was such a damn likable man. Could he be trusted? She recalled a rookie student at the academy who had gotten her trust and then ended up embarrassing her badly in front of the whole class. She couldn't afford to have that happen here. No, she would be living in this town and working here. She couldn't make those kinds of mistakes any longer.

"I'll try," was all she could promise.

Gil's brows moved downward in displeasure. "You'd better try real hard then," he growled.

Back at the station they cleaned their turnout gear and hung it back up. Then the engine and the squad truck were washed and lovingly dried by hand. Leah ignored the curious looks of her teammates, embarrassed enough by her chance injury without elaborating on it. The other three fire fighters talked about the wreck among themselves, excluding her from the conversation. She choked down the hurt, biting on her lower lip, and finished wiping the windshield on the squad truck. Gil had disappeared and she was sure he was filling out the fire reports which the police and the insurance companies would be demanding by the next morning.

As Leah saw the camaraderie that the firemen shared, an ache began in her heart. Couldn't they at least be civil and say a few words to her? Instead, they completely ignored her, making her feel even more miserable than she already felt. Her head was aching fiercely and she went upstairs to the bunk room, rearranging her boots and bunker pants by her bed. She rummaged around in the small bathroom for some aspirin, but found none. She went back downstairs in search of Gil. At the office door she knocked timidly.

"Come on in," he invited.

Leah poked her head around the corner. "I'm sorry to bother you, but I'd like to take some aspirin. Where are they kept?"

Gil glanced up, his eyes darkening as he studied her. "The chief keeps them in his office. I'll get you some. Hang on." He returned with two white tablets and placed them in her opened hand. "You look pale," he observed, going back to the desk and sitting down.

She masked the turmoil of her feelings. "I'll live."

"If you're done with the bay work, go take a shower. Maybe you'll feel better then," he suggested easily.

"Yeah, maybe," she agreed.

By the time she took a hot shower and washed her hair, it was close to six a.m. The other firemen waited until she was done before trudging upstairs. As Leah made her bunk she could hear them laughing and trading stories while they showered. Hurriedly, she went back downstairs to the kitchen, leaving the bunk room empty so that they could come out wearing their towels or whatever. At eight o'clock they went off duty and she longed to go home and simply fall onto that double bed in her apartment and sleep the sleep of the dead.

Looking for something to keep her occupied, she made fresh coffee and then turned on the television set and sat down. Apache was the first to wander in, his hair dark and gleaming from the recent shower. He sniffed.

"Hey...that fresh coffee brewing?"

Leah lifted her head. "Yes."

He gave her a measuring look. "Made it all on your own?"

"With my own two hands," she promised.

"Man, there's nothing like a cup of fresh hot coffee and a cigarette after a run. Thanks, Stevenson...."

She frowned. Well, she'd just have to get used to them using her last name. At least Apache was being sociable, and she took it as a major step forward in her relationship with the Italian fire fighter.

Sam and Duke eventually sauntered in, murmuring their surprise over the newly made coffee. Sam gave her a nod of thanks but Duke said nothing, making a point of sitting as far away from her as he could. There was an unnatural silence in the room and Leah wanted to squirm. If she weren't there, they'd be bantering back and forth, joking and laughing. She couldn't stand the tense atmosphere one moment longer, so she stood, then walked back out into the bay, taking a long breath of air. Leaning against the squad, she watched as the sun rose above the hills east of the city, her coffee cup balanced on the fender of the truck.

She heard the men laughing loudly at someone's joke. Rubbing her forehead gently, she tried to will the headache away.

"Think you're up to going to Cleveland today?"

Leah gasped, spinning around. Coffee

sloshed over the rim of the cup, scalding her hand.

"Sorry," Gil proffered.

"That's all right. I'm just a little jumpy."

He rested against the fender, watching her through half-closed eyes. "It's going to take a while before they get used to having you around," he said, turning and listening to the fire fighters' noisy laughter. "They're just as nervous as you. Only they show it in a different way."

She managed a weak smile. "I came out here to the bay to give them breathing room so they could tell jokes or swear."

"Well, in case you haven't noticed yet, the swearing gets thick and heavy when we've got a bad call. Just shut your ears and pretend you don't hear it," he advised good-naturedly.

"A little swearing is good for the soul."

He cocked his head. "You mean you mouth a few good ones in a crisis?" he teased.

"You bet. I'll probably let go one of these days soon and their ears will burn," she answered. Leah felt inexplicably comfortable with Gil. She knew she shouldn't. He was the officer in charge and she was only a fire fighter.

"I think they can handle it. Are you feeling up to getting some equipment that fits you this morning, or do you want to do it tomorrow?"

"We've got the next forty-eight hours off. How about Thursday? It will give me a chance to try and complete my move into the apartment."

He rubbed his strong jaw. "Just give me your address and a time and I'll pick you up."

Leah walked with him over to the office and sat down. She wrote out her address and new phone number while he lounged on the corner of the desk. "How about eleven?"

"Sounds good." He looked at the paper. "You're living right on the city limits I see. There's a good volunteer station in the neighboring township that's looking for more people. Interested?"

She groaned. "Listen, I've got my hands full just fitting in here, Lieutenant. I don't need to take on a volunteer department full of men at the same time."

"I don't blame you. Too bad."

"Why?"

"Oh, I'm on duty over there on my off days."

"You're a volunteer in your spare time?" she asked, stunned.

"Sure."

"Oh." Leah had thought a wife might be responsible for occupying his time off. "You're sure a glutton for punishment. Doesn't our chief object to your doing it?"

"No. Remember, I was a volunteer long before I got here."

She looked up into his amused face. There was a blend of humor and gentleness evident in his eyes and she felt completely relaxed around him. "You must love fighting fires."

"Mmm, I do enjoy it, but the real fact is they need people during the day. Most volunteer departments are terribly understaffed for day fires. Well, when things settle down around here, maybe you'll give it a second thought."

"Will they be just as against women fire fighters as they are here?" she asked, unable to keep the bitterness out of her voice.

"I doubt it. You're coming from a paid department and they know you've got the training hours. And if there is some resentment, they'll never confront you with it."

"'No, just talk a lot behind my back.''

''Did they do that down at the academy?''

She nodded her head dolefully. ''The rookies did. Why can't they accept or reject me on my ability and not my sex?''

''Because you're an oddity,'' Gil murmured. He gave her an encouraging smile. ''Let's face it, only about one percent of the one million three hundred thousand firemen in the U.S. are women. You're bucking some strong statistics.''

''I'm bucking straight chauvinism out of the eighteen hundreds,'' she shot back more strongly than she intended.

''Only time will make the difference,'' he said philosophically. ''If I'm not being too nosy, why did you become a fire fighter?''

''Because I wanted to make a contribution to my community. I know it sounds corny, but it's the truth.''

''It doesn't sound corny.''

''I guess it all started when I was an air controller.'' She gave him a searching look. ''Do you know what I mean? Like that guy we extricated from the wreck. We saved his life. How many occupations give you that kind of responsibility? How many times can we be in a position to be at the right place and time and be useful in a life-or-death situation?'' Her voice took on a fervency she normally squelched. ''I don't know, I'm beginning to think there's something drastically wrong with my emotional makeup,'' she muttered.

Gil shook his head. ''From my view, there's nothing wrong with you emotionally. I prefer a woman who is independent and can stand on her own two feet.''

''Well, you're in a class by yourself, then. Most men would like to see my kind banished to some desert island. And yet, they think nothing of a man performing the same services.'' She gave an explosive laugh. ''Figure it out. God made men and women equal when it came to feelings and emotions. If a man can do it, why can't a woman?''

''You won't get an argument out of me,'' he said, grinning. ''You know, not only do you have honesty, you've got intelligence. I knew that sparkle in your eyes meant something.''

Leah blushed becomingly beneath his praise. ''I try and hide that side of myself.''

"Why?"

"Because if I were my real self around here, I'd never be accepted."

"And who is the real Leah?" he asked.

She hesitated, suddenly losing some of her natural ebullience. "With your insight, you'll probably find out soon enough," she replied.

"I'll be looking forward to taking you up to Cleveland on Thursday, then," he said, rousing himself. "In the meantime, take care of yourself." He halted as he approached her and lightly brushed her cheek. "You've got a beauty of a black eye, lady."

A small shiver of delight made her skin tingle where he had briefly touched her. There was a gentleness about Gil Gerard that drew her like a moth to an open flame. But he could be just as dangerous to her as that flame, she reminded herself. It had only been a year since she'd left her marriage behind, and the painful memories still made her hesitant about trusting any man.

Jack Danielson had been a fighter pilot in the air force and she had fallen for his exotic and exciting image. Later, after a year of marriage, Leah had found that the man beneath the image was not what she'd expected. Now, she wanted only to forget those six years of misery. Jack's need to chase other women had left her disillusioned with marriage. Sometimes she still questioned her own sexuality and wondered if she had been partially responsible for his unfaithfulness.

Leah closed her eyes tightly against the pain of her memories. She had stopped at the bay doors, and when she opened her eyes again, she stared sightlessly at the awakening city.

Rubbing her throbbing forehead, she thought about the last year of her marriage. Jack had been frank in his dissatisfaction with their sex life. What had happened to the passionate expressiveness she had exhibited during the first four years of their marriage? What had turned her off? A part of it was discovering Jack's tryst with the wife of another officer on base and his laughing admission that there had been others. Every time he held her in his arms, she froze. He had then accused her of using sex to punish him and she had sobbed until there were no more tears left. Had she? And was Jack right when he accused her of being maladjusted because she wanted to hold down a man's job?

She had always known she was different and had reluctantly accepted that fact about herself. But after years of snide remarks and barbed comments from both men and women, she was getting tired of her uniqueness. She was beginning to long to fit in. Yet after getting an honorable discharge from the air force and her divorce papers from Jack, she had again chosen an occupation that was different. God, am I a glutton for punishment? she wondered in anguish. Was Jack right? Is there something psychologically wrong with me?

Leah's feeling of depression continued after the chief brusquely dismissed them. The bay, engines, and bunk room had passed inspection, and now the fire fighters were allowed to go home and rest for two days before taking on another twenty-fours of grueling duty. She drove home slowly, still immersed in her thoughts. Isn't there someone in this world who will accept me as I am? she wondered miserably. Why couldn't I have been like everyone else? Be a sheep and be accepted. She smiled grimly. "Be unique and be an outcast," she muttered aloud.

* * *

She didn't know how long she had slept, but a persistent knock at the apartment door dragged her to a state of semiwakefulness. Her head ached abominably as she sat up, groping to throw the covers off her. What time was it? It was dark as she stumbled through the bedroom. After managing to pull her maroon robe over her shoulders, Leah fumbled with the sash at the waist.

"Just a minute...." she called. God, her nose hurt and the pain in her brow was increasing. Holding one hand against her forehead, Leah leaned down and turned on a small table lamp in the living room. Finally she got to the door and opened it. Gil Gerard stood there in a navy blue polo shirt and a pair of well-worn jeans. Her eyes widened and her heart began to beat erratically as she stared up at him.

Seconds fled by, but it seemed like minutes. Her first thought was that she must look disheveled, with her dark walnut-colored hair cascading over her shoulders. The pain in her brow intensified, bringing tears to her eyes.

"I just stopped by to see how you were," Gil said by way of explanation. "I called three different times and you didn't answer the phone. I got worried."

Touching her temple in a nervous gesture, she turned and motioned him to come in. "I'm sorry," she said, her voice husky with sleep. "I've got to sit down...."

Leah was aware of the door closing as she sat, her head in the hollow of her hands. Her heart beat heavily in her breast. The concern in Gil's voice was genuine and she didn't know how to respond to it. How long had it been since a man cared about her on a personal level? Too long, a voice cried deep within her. She felt his hand on her shoulder as he knelt at her side.

"You look like you're in a lot of pain," he said, studying her with renewed intensity.

His fingers were warm as they rested upon the thin material covering her shoulder. Instinctively, Leah responded to his gentleness. "I've got an awful headache."

"How long since you had some aspirin?"

She shrugged. "I don't remember. As soon as I got home I went to bed." Looking up, she felt her heart contract with new emotions. Gil was only inches away. His knee rested comfortably against her thigh, sending a pleasurable shock through her body. His eyes were hooded and unreadable. "What time is it, anyway?" she asked.

"Eight p.m. You've slept a long time," he observed. He reached out with his right hand and carefully brushed several strands of hair from her brow. "Here, let me take a look at that nose," he commanded, slipping his hand beneath her chin.

His touch was electrifying and she inhaled sharply. His fingers were strong and yet, at the same moment, tender. Idiotically, Leah wondered what it would be like to be loved by Gil. That thought created even more havoc in her responsive body. She watched as his mouth thinned.

"Let me get you a warm cloth to put across the bridge," he said. "Maybe it will take down some of the swelling. Stay here. I'll get the aspirin," he ordered.

"But—" she began lamely as he rose to his full height.

"No arguments," he said, looking down at

her. ''And I don't care if you're not used to being taken care of.''

Gratefully, she fell back against the couch, her mind wandering aimlessly while she waited for him. A minute later Gil came back with two aspirin and a glass of water. After she took them he settled down beside her, carefully placing the warm cloth against her nose and cheeks.

''Thanks,'' she offered, feeling almost immediate relief with the application of heat.

He grinned for the first time. ''My pleasure.''

''I haven't unpacked everything yet, but there's a coffeepot in the kitchen.''

He raised an eyebrow. ''Feel like a cup of coffee?''

''No...but I thought you might. I just feel too lousy to get up and make it for you,'' she returned wryly.

Placing his hand on her shoulder, he said, ''It's about time you started taking care of yourself first instead of last.''

Leah gave him a confused look. Just his touch sent her mind reeling. His maleness was evident in the way he walked, the magnificent shape of his body, and the deep timbre of his voice. She trembled, finding herself shy in his presence. "I don't know what you mean."

Gil felt the tension in her shoulder muscles and began to gently massage the area. The softness of the material made it easy to move his hand in small circles on her shoulders and upper back. At first she stiffened against his ministrations. "Take it easy," he coaxed. "You're tight as a drum. Don't you ever relax?" he asked, a smile softening his words.

She gave him a confused look. "I—sure I do...but—"

He laughed ruefully. "Here, turn around with your back toward me. Let's work out some of those kinks. Your neck is so stiff that it's probably contributing to your headache."

Leah hesitated, searching his guileless features. Was he playing a game? And why? Her mind was balking but her heart cried out for his continued touch. "Well—"

"Stubborn lady," he growled, moving her so he could work on her. Gently, he forced the muscles in her back to relax beneath his coaxing hands. He bore down, monitoring the amount of pressure as his fingers slid across her shoulders. Leah tried to remain tense, but it was impossible. He was working magic on her taut body and a sigh escaped from her lips.

"That feels so good," she murmured, arching against his hands.

"You're like a cat getting stroked," he said softly. "You really are in good shape." He traced the curve of her spine with both thumbs. "You have a beautiful back," he murmured.

Leah dissolved against him. Miraculously, her headache disappeared and she placed the cloth on her lap, arching shamelessly into his kneading hands. It was magic, she thought blissfully. He was magic! Without meaning to, she gave herself totally to his masterful hands.

"That's better," he murmured huskily.

Ten minutes beneath his hands erased her distrustful thoughts. Gil eased her down on the couch, then went into the bathroom and warmed up the cloth again. After fifteen more minutes, the swelling was reduced and the pain in her nose had almost disappeared. He sat beside her, his arm draped casually behind her head, a pleased expression on his face. "Better?" he inquired.

Even the tone of his voice was balm to her senses. "Much. I owe you one, Gil. Thanks."

Deviltry danced in his eyes. "Don't worry, lady, I intend to collect," he murmured. "Do you feel up to eating something before you hit the sack again?"

Her stomach was growling rather loudly and she placed her hand self-consciously over that part of her body. "I guess I am."

He roused himself. "Got any food in the refrigerator yet?"

"Yes, but I think all I could eat right now is a salad."

"Sounds good. Why don't you stretch out on the couch and rest while I make us dinner."

Leah didn't refuse his offer. "Sounds good," she agreed tiredly. Stretched out on the couch, she soon fell into a light sleep while Gil rummaged around in the kitchen.

Half an hour later, Gil ambled into the living room, wiping his hands on a towel. He halted a few feet from where Leah lay sleeping. Her face was relaxed and devoid of that usual defensive mask she wore like armor. He allowed his hands to drop to his sides as he approached the couch. There was a vulnerability in her sleeping features that he hadn't seen before. He sat down on the edge of the couch, his body brushing against hers, and lightly caressed her flushed cheek. Her flesh was smooth and warm beneath his hand. She was beautiful despite her injury. Leaning over, he caressed her parted lips with his mouth. Her lips were like lovely flower petals to be explored, tasted, and outlined. Gil felt her respond, felt her lips return the pressure of his mouth.

As she awoke, Leah was excruciatingly aware of his maleness, of the muscular hardness of his thigh against her hip. His mouth worshiped her lips. Warmth uncurled quickly from the center of her body as the pressure of his mouth increased against her parted lips. The natural male scent of his body and the tantalizing taste of his mouth combined to make her giddy with excitement.

A soft moan rose in her throat as he deepened the kiss, his tongue invading the depths of her, stroking each hollow with masterful insistence. She melted beneath him, her arms automatically sliding across his broad, powerful shoulders.

Consumed by the molten heat of his kiss, Leah reveled in the primitive desires he had released within her.

Finally, he raised his head, his face inches from her own. His eyes were a dark blue, silvered with barely contained passion. Her breath was coming fast and shallow as she stared wide-eyed up into his face. Her heart thundered in her ears and she was aware that her breasts were taut beneath the lush fabric of her robe. An ache was beginning in her lower body and she yearned to continue the magical interlude. Never had she been awakened from sleep by such a kiss. Never had a man aroused her so strongly.

Gil broke the silence, his face thoughtful and composed in the semidarkness. "I didn't mean to do that," he murmured, his voice husky with desire. "You looked so damn beautiful sleeping there...your lips..." He took a steadying breath. "You're one hell of a woman. And if you weren't injured I wouldn't have stopped with just a kiss."

Her heart thrilled to his admission. "It was a lovely way to wake up," she admitted, her voice barely audible.

Gil gave her a sheepish smile and straightened up. "Feel like walking to the kitchen or would you like me to bring dinner to you?"

"No, I'll get up." Just the firm grip of his fingers on her arm sent a quiver through her. How could he make her feel both vulnerable and feminine at the same time? How long had it been since she'd felt like a woman in a man's arms? Too long, a voice whispered. Too long. Gil seated her, bringing over a large bowl of salad.

"That's enough for a horse!" she protested, laughing.

He grinned boyishly. "Lady, you need some meat on those bones. You're too damn skinny. Go on, eat all of it," he instructed.

Leah felt her face growing warm beneath his gaze. "What do you think I am, a rabbit?" she teased, picking up her fork.

Gil sat down opposite her with an even larger salad than the one he had fixed for her. Pouring a liberal dose of creamy Italian dressing on it, he smiled. "You're hardly a rabbit. A good-looking woman with one hell of a body, but definitely not a rabbit." A wicked gleam came to his eyes as he caught her startled gaze. "I'd say you were more like a lioness. I liked the way you purred earlier when I was massaging you. We ought to do that again sometime."

Caught off guard by his easy banter, Leah didn't know what to say. Instead, she picked at her salad.

Later, over coffee in the living room, Gil chose to sit on a chair opposite the couch, where Leah was sitting. He sensed that she was still shaken by their kiss and he cursed himself for moving too quickly with her. From the moment he'd met her in the office, Leah Stevenson had affected him strongly. Without appearing hurried, he finished off his coffee.

"Well," he noted, satisfaction in his voice, "you look like you'll live now. I've got to drop in at the volunteer fire department, so I'll get going." He rose, giving her a warm smile.

"Thanks for coming over, Gil. No, I mean it. Don't give me that look."

His blue eyes sparkled with mirth. "I want you to know I don't normally go around kissing ladies after knowing them only a day."

"At least I didn't turn into a frog," she teased, getting to her feet.

Gil laughed deeply as he placed his cup and saucer on the draining board. ‘‘I may not be a prince, but lady, you sure as hell are a princess. A very brave, courageous one at that.’’ He walked over, his face revealing his happiness. ‘‘How about if I pick you up about ten tomorrow morning and we'll get you a pair of boots that fit?’’

Leah breathed deeply. She could smell his natural body scent and it was like inhaling some long-lost perfume. ‘‘Yes,’’ she murmured, ‘‘that would be fine.’’ Automatically she reached out and put her hand on his arm. ‘‘And more important, Gil, thanks for coming over to check up on me. I never expected that—’’

He leaned over and placed a kiss on her hair. ‘‘Strictly a selfish gesture on my part,’’ he said. His eyes became more serious as he studied her upturned face. ‘‘Now, if you have any problems, I've left my phone number on the telephone stand for you. Call if you need me. Okay?’’

She dropped her gaze, shaking her head. ‘‘Do you know how long it's been since someone genuinely cared whether I lived or died?’’ she asked softly. "I don't mean to sound like I'm complaining or can't take the pressure of my job." Her eyes were dark and glistening with unshed tears as she met his concerned gaze. "You've earned my respect, Gil."

He ran his fingers lightly along her cheek. "I intend to earn more than that. Get some sleep," he urged huskily. "I'll see you in the morning."

Three

A simmering excitement coursed through Leah as she hesitated in front of the closet. Morning had come quickly and she fingered the recently unpacked clothes, wondering what to wear. The feminine side of herself wanted to wear a dress. But who went to buy fire boots in a dress? She reluctantly settled on a lavender blouse edged with small ruffles around the throat, and a pair of white slacks. After slipping into her sandals, she went to the bedroom mirror and released her hair so that it flowed across her shoulders.

Leah tried to assess herself honestly in the mirror. She touched her full mouth, gazing soberly into her large green eyes. What did Gil see in her? She wasn't pretty by modeling standards. Walnut-colored lashes framed her jade and gold eyes, giving them the appearance of being slightly tilted at the corners. Her oval face was marked by a strong chin. Her nose was straight and clean and she fondly remembered her mother telling her it was the mark of an aristocrat. She had gone through grade school thinking she had the greatest nose in the world until other kids began to make fun of her "Roman" nose. From then on she had hung around with the boys on the softball team because they didn't care what she looked like, as long as she hit home runs.

The doorbell rang, bringing her out of the reverie, and Leah quickly applied her lipstick. Her heart picked up a beat as she opened the door. Gil nodded genially. He was dressed in a white polo shirt and a pair of tan slacks. He looked devastatingly handsome to her, the width of his broad shoulders swallowing up the space in the doorway.

"Come on in," she said breathlessly. "I'm almost ready."

One eyebrow raised as he drank in her form. "Lady, you look absolutely beautiful," he said appreciatively.

Leah turned, startled by the genuine awe in his husky voice. To cover up her surprise, she grimaced. "That and fifty cents will get you a cup of coffee," she answered flippantly as she went to the bedroom to pick up her shoulder bag. When she came out, he was frowning.

"I don't make a habit of complimenting a woman unless I think it's deserved. So take the compliment and say thank you."

She was speechless. He had a sensitivity that made her want to know more about Gil Gerard the man, not the fire fighter. "Thank you," she blurted, embarrassed by her flippant approach.

The weather was warm and breezy, and the gentle wind lifted strands of hair playfully about her shoulders as they walked along the terrace outside her apartment. He gave her a warm smile, following her down the steps. "It's lucky you can't wear your hair like that at the fire station. All I'd do is watch you—I'd never get any work done."

"Where did you pick up that diploma in blarney?" she demanded.

He caught up with her at the bottom, matching her stride as he directed her to the red pickup at the end of the parking lot. "The same place you got your diploma in dodging compliments."

Leah glanced up at him and caught the merriment lurking in his eyes. "Touché."

"Want to start over?"

"Sure." He opened the door for her and she stopped, grinning. "Is this standard procedure or are you just trying to impress me?"

Gil returned the smile. "Both. When I'm off duty there are some things I still like to do for a woman. And opening doors is one of them." He gave her a wicked look. "Maybe you'll get a chance to sample some of the others, too."

Leah ignored the innuendo. She slid in and buckled up the safety belt. After having extricated victims who hadn't used seat belts, she found it was second nature to take the precaution. Gil went through the same procedure and drove the truck out to the main road, where he made a right turn. She relaxed, feeling better than she had in months. When had she felt so free? So happy?

He turned to glance at her. "No one would ever guess you were a woman fire fighter the way you're dressed today. If those guys down at the station could see me with you, they'd drool with envy."

Leah couldn't help laughing. "Do you always say the right thing, Gil Gerard, or did you memorize the list before you came to pick me up?"

"Neither. I just happen to believe in honesty and positive reinforcement."

"I see. Positive strokes instead of negative ones. Well, that's probably why you're such a good fire officer. You say the right thing at the right time to get the best performance out of people."

He shrugged. "Maybe. I wasn't born with it, you know. I've learned a lot about people over the years."

"So have I."

"Oh? What did you learn?"

She hesitated and then blurted, "That I'm a misfit, I suppose."

"Hmm, why do you say it with such distaste? I like the fact that you're different."

She laughed, covering her bitterness. "I'm a maverick, in case you haven't noticed. I don't belong in a woman's world and I don't belong in a man's."

Gil shrugged. If he was affected by her sudden seriousness and the pain evident in her voice, he made no sign of it. Instead he smiled. "You're one of the new breed of women, Leah. And I would think that being a leader in that sense has some pretty heavy emotional responsibilities. And you know something? I think your kind is a pretty interesting and provocative addition. You have brains, aggressiveness, and good looks to boot. Not a bad combination for someone who calls herself a misfit."

"Then you're as much a misfit as I am if you're so gung ho on the new breed of women," she growled, trying to recover from his point-blank compliment.

"I sort of enjoy being myself," he said mildly. Then, as if sensing her discomfort, he switched topics. "Any more nosebleeds since last night?"

"No, I'm fine today."

"Good. You didn't deserve that punch in the nose after doing such a good job the first time out with us."

"Do you ever say a nasty thing to anyone?" she asked disbelievingly.

He laughed heartily. "Sure, ask the men down at the station. I'm not all sweetness and light."

Leah could accept that. She remembered the night of the wreck and the quiet confidence that had emanated from Gil like a beacon of light. Today, however, he was in a teasing mood and would not apologize for it in any way. Maybe she had been under too much pressure for too long. In her effort to make the grade as a fire fighter, she had had no time to enjoy life. It came as a shock that she had forgotten how to laugh, to tease, to joke. She met Gil's gaze and felt another heavy load slip off her shoulders.

"You must think I'm the most sour woman in the world," she said softly in apology.

"I think you've been under a hell of a strain having to prove yourself down at the academy, go through the nightmare of a court battle to get this job, and now face a third test with the people here at the fire department. It isn't any wonder you don't smile very often or laugh. I wouldn't either under those circumstances."

"You don't scare easy, do you, Gil?"

His blue eyes were lively with challenge. "No. Should I be scared of you?"

Leah forced a weak smile. "Listen, with my track record you're better off keeping your distance." She didn't mean to sound hard and brittle.

"Let me be the judge of that," he returned, catching the anguish in her eyes. "Mind if I pry a little about your past?" he asked softly.

She looked away, unable to stand the compassion in his gaze. Folding her hands tightly in her lap, she muttered, "Am I that transparent?"

"Don't worry, I won't give away any of your secrets. They're safe with me."

"You're scaring me, Gil. I'd swear you're reading my mind."

"Just your pretty green eyes."

She moaned, leaning back against the seat and closing her eyes for a moment. "My God, am I that readable? What if the guys down at the station see—''

''Listen to me, Leah. I happen to make a habit of watching eyes, and I can see and read things in them that most people haven't taken the time to look for. No psychic ability, just plain watching on my part. Okay?''

''I guess I have to start learning to trust someone again,'' she admitted hesitantly.

''I trusted you out there at the accident and you didn't let me down. What we talk about between ourselves stays with us. I won't say anything to the men at the station, I promise.''

''You don't know how hard it is for me to trust, Gil. Down at the academy I thought I could trust certain firemen and I found out the hard way that I couldn't.''

''Have you ever trusted any man?''

The knife in her heart twisted and tears blurred her vision. ''You have the damndest way of asking the right question,'' she admitted, her voice barely above a whisper.

''I can see the pain in your eyes. I figure you got hurt pretty bad by a man. Right?''

''Right.''

"And not too long ago, judging by your defensiveness."

She stared at him. "Isn't anything hidden from you?" she demanded, awed by his insight.

Gil grinned broadly. "Plenty, lady. But I'm going to enjoy making those little discoveries about you as time goes on," he promised huskily.

"How about my discovering a little bit about you?" she demanded, surprised at her audacity.

He smiled. "Sure, anything you want to know."

Leah gave him a black look. "Must be nice to be an open book with everyone."

"Jealousy will get you nowhere. But don't think I'm this way with everyone. Just certain special people."

She fought against the pleasure she took in his last comment. How could he be so sure that there was something special between them? It puzzled her and she lapsed into momentary silence.

"Well?" Gil prompted. "Go ahead."

"I find it hard to believe you aren't married. You're good-looking, intelligent, and have a secure job."

His blue eyes sparkled. ''And you're wondering why the women aren't knocking down the door, right?''

''Right.''

He shrugged. ''Let's put it this way, Leah, it takes a very special woman to fulfill certain requirements I've set.''

''Such as?''

He lost some of his merriment and drove for at least another mile before answering. ''Not every woman has courage, Leah. Like I told you before, I admire that quality. I'm not looking for an aggressive, masculine type of woman. But someone who isn't afraid to use her brains and talents.''

Leah turned in the seat, resting her back against the door. ''You've been married before.'' It was a statement, not a question.

Gil pursed his lips and nodded. ''Yes...yes, I was,'' he admitted softly.

Leah gave him a strange look; she had the feeling that she was treading on very unstable ground with him. She couldn't understand why any woman would divorce him. ''She must have been crazy to leave you, then,'' she said.

The strained atmosphere in the cab became almost palpable. Leah felt her stomach knotting. Had she made a horrible gaffe? Anxiously, she searched his face. There was pain in his eyes as he regarded her through those thick black lashes. "I'm sorry," she said quickly, "I shouldn't have said that. I—"

"It's all right," he soothed, reaching out and briefly covering her hand with his own. "It's a pretty sad story, Leah, but I don't mind telling you about it if you want to know." His features were serious as he squeezed her hand.

A pleasurable tingle fled up her arm and she was once again struck by the controlled strength of his fingers. "If you're willing to share it with me, I would like to know."

"I got married when I was twenty-four, Leah. I had known Jenny two years before we decided to make a go of it. She wasn't very happy about me doing fire fighting."

"Many wives aren't," Leah noted.

"That was one of the things that kept us from getting married sooner," he murmured, shaking his head. "Jenny was frail healthwise, but she had a backbone of steel." His voice lowered.

"And I didn't realize just how much of a fighter she was until she contracted leukemia."

Leah gasped softly, her eyes widening. "Oh, no!"

Gil's lips thinned, as if he were recalling that period in his life. "That happened a long time ago," he said. "She fought it for five years before dying."

She wanted to reach out and comfort him. The anguish in his voice was strong even now. "How long ago was that?"

"Three years. On some days it seems like yesterday. On other days it seems like it happened a hundred years ago."

Leah felt her heart contract with pain. "I didn't think you were the type of man to give up on a relationship," she murmured, almost to herself.

He managed a crooked smile. "Loyal to the end, that's true. What about you, Leah? I think you're too good-looking to have run around single all this time."

She took a deep, unsteady breath and folded her hands tightly in her lap. "I don't have a very good track record, I'm afraid."

"'You don't have to tell me now, but I'd honestly like to understand your background.''

"'You mean how I developed my distrust of all men plus the chip on my shoulder?'' she countered nervously. Would he understand, a voice asked? Suddenly, Leah cared a great deal what Gil thought of her. She clenched her fingers a little tighter together.

"'Let me tell you a little story,'' Gil responded. "'It might make you feel better about telling me about your past. I own a farm outside of town where I keep a couple of horses. I left the city life behind after Jenny died and headed for the country. I didn't know much about horses but I'd always wanted to own some. A local horse trader found out I was looking for a pair and sold me two part Arabians. I knew I was in trouble when one of them, a gray mare, nearly tore the horse trailer apart when they unloaded her. The dealer hadn't bothered to mention that the horse had been badly abused and was sour on people.

"'I had time on my hands because I was still grieving for Jenny. Instead of forcing the dealer to take the mare back, I decided to try and work with her. She had been badly beaten a number of times and she distrusted any man who came within fifty feet of her.'' He shook his head, his voice becoming softer. "I used kindness and love to tame her down. Today she's an outgoing mare who loves women and kids. She's still nervous around men, but a couple years ago no one could get near her without getting kicked or bitten.'' He glanced over at her. ''So you see, even if you have that so-called chip on your shoulder and a distrust of men, it doesn't scare me. You remind me of my mare, Leah. You've been badly hurt and you're trying your damndest to keep your head above the pain and survive.''

She fought back her tears. ''Like I said,'' she forced out, her throat constricted, ''nothing seems to scare you off.''

He grinned. ''Not when I consider someone worthy of my attention and concern. So tell me, what happened back there to make you run so scared, Lady?''

He made the admission easy. By the time they arrived in Cleveland an hour later, she had told him of Jack and his affairs. Gil had remained quiet and attentive throughout the conversation, occasionally reaching out to touch her hand. Each time he did, the urge to cry welled up within her. They sat there in the parked truck, the sun pouring brightly into the cab. Gil roused himself.

"You've made a hell of a comeback, Leah, despite some pretty long odds. You've got what it takes." There was a new note of admiration in his voice.

"I'm trying very hard not to allow my feelings for Jack to interfere with the guys at the department. Duke hates me and I find myself getting defensive and snapping back at him." She gave him a doleful look. "That isn't good, Gil. Duke won't trust me out at a fire scene and I don't trust him."

He squeezed her hand. "I wish you had told me this before, but it isn't too late to start correcting the situation."

A lump formed in her throat. "I don't want to cause trouble!"

"Duke is just going to have to learn to handle his prejudice," he said grimly, opening the door. He gave her a devastating smile.

"Come on, pretty lady, we've got a pair of boots to buy for you. A pair of glass slippers for my princess."

Leah hesitantly allowed herself to be drawn into his sudden ebullient mood. As she walked with him toward the store, she felt another bit of the weight she had been carrying since the divorce slip free of her aching shoulders. Stealing a glance up at Gil, she tried not to examine too closely how she felt about him. They barely knew each other, and yet it seemed like they had known each other forever....

Four

Leah had hoped that by the time her first two months of duty had gone by there would be a change in Duke Saxon's attitude. Unfortunately, though the other men had warmed to her, Duke remained as hostile as ever.

She stepped into the front door of the firehouse, giving the dispatcher, Bill Colby, a warm smile. She was looking forward to seeing Gil on duty. She had noted a change in Gil's attitude as far as she was concerned. It was as if he sensed her need to approach any new relationship slowly. Since that wonderful day in Cleveland, he had not asked her for a date.

She made her way to the kitchen and started preparing the menu for the day, since it was her turn. She hummed to herself, realizing that she was happy. Despite Duke's stubborn attitude, everyone at the firehouse was adjusting to having a woman fire fighter aboard. She had to admit that her performance at fire scenes had helped to cement the trust between her and the men.

Chief Anders came hurrying by, gave her a brief nod, and resumed his pace, hands behind his back. She smiled to herself as she prepared a simple Yankee pot roast, complete with carrots, onion, and plenty of potatoes for Saxon, who seemed to live on them. After putting it in the refrigerator to be baked later in the day, she had just set about making fresh coffee when Gil ambled in. He smiled over at her.

"You look like a regular house Frau," he teased as he sat down at the table and spread out some paperwork before him.

Her face was damp from working over a hot stove and tendrils of hair clung to her cheek.

Leah returned the smile as she brushed the strands of hair away. "Believe it or not, I enjoy cooking."

"Don't let the guys hear you say that or you'll become a permanent fixture in here." He motioned for her to sit down. "How's that burn on your neck?"

She automatically reached up, touching it carefully. Three days earlier she had received the injury at a house fire. "It stings a little, that's all. Part of my dues for being part of the fire service."

"Great welcome," he snorted, riffling through a pile of reports.

She sat there in companionable silence with him for a few minutes before initiating a conversation. "Gil, how did you know that front door was going to blow?" she asked, referring to the incident in which she'd been burned.

He raised his head, meeting her troubled gaze. "I saw the glass bowing outward. The windows in the other rooms weren't as bad, so I just put two and two together. The heat from the kitchen traveled to the foyer area first. I suppose you're kicking yourself for not noticing it?" he asked dryly.

"Yes. I was taught to look for downed electrical wires in yards, windows bowing outward, and to approach a door from the side. Never walk up to it like I did."

"Ten lashes with a wet noodle."

"Come on, it was a bad mistake!" she flared, folding her hands tightly on the table.

"It could have been but it wasn't. It taught you a good lesson—you'll never make that mistake again."

"You got that right," she returned fervently, shaking her head at her own stupidity.

"Quit being so hard on yourself. You let me worry about rating your abilities. If I say you did a good job, just say thanks." He tapped her arm gently. "I'm finding out you have one hell of a time taking a compliment. You take an insult much easier."

She eyed him suspiciously. "I always look a gift horse in the mouth. Particularly when it's a man giving me the compliment."

"Not every male has an ulterior motive, Leah."

Her mouth stretched into a grin. "Oh?"

His eyes danced with silent laughter. "Well,

maybe some have positive ulterior motives instead of negative ones.''

''I can buy that.''

He resumed his paperwork and she got up to pull down two mugs from the pegboard behind the sink. ''Want coffee?'' she asked.

''Please.''

Leah returned to her chair, sipping the hot black liquid. It startled her how comfortable she felt around Gil. His easygoing nature had made all the difference in the world for her at the fire station. What would she have done if she hadn't found someone like him here? Could she have endured the loneliness?

''Here, this just came off the mimeograph,'' he said, handing her a flier.

Leah read it. ''A department picnic next Sunday?''

''Yup. The chief throws it once a year. All the fire fighters and their families get together over at the local park. It ought to be a lot of fun. There's swimming in the lake, softball, sack races for the kids, and good food.''

She glanced at him. ''I haven't met a male fire fighter yet who didn't think of his stomach first.''

Gil smiled. "Listen, lady, being a bachelor now is hell on my digestive system. I get lucky when you cook here or when one of the wives takes pity on us and brings a home-cooked meal to the station. This picnic is a chance to get some more of that good food."

Leah rolled her eyes. "You are so typically male!"

He joined her laughter. "If there are any left-overs from tonight's meal, can I take them home in a doggy bag? It's better than pulling out another frozen dinner on my day off."

She stared at him in disbelief. "You can't be serious!"

He shrugged. "Well, it's either that or just flat out ask you to invite me over for dinner some night."

"And here I was feeling sorry for you. Just an elaborate trick to get an invitation."

Gil rose, shuffling the finished paperwork together. "I could be cruel and invite you over to my house for beans and wieners. Then you'd make sure to invite me for dinner next time."

A new joyous feeling enveloped her as she sat looking up at him. He had such a mobile, expressive face when he allowed that official mask to drop away. Leah held his gaze.

"Well?" he prodded.

"What?"

"Do I get the invitation?"

"Why don't you reserve your options until after this meal," she teased. "Like Duke says, I could poison you all."

"Apache does a good job of that," he countered with feeling. "I for one am glad to see a woman in the kitchen here. At least we eat decently when you draw the low card in the deck."

She stood and pushed her chair back up to the table. "Why do I get the feeling that you're going to try and rig the deck to make sure I cook most of the time?"

He tossed a smile over his shoulder as he walked out. "I wouldn't do anything like that."

"Bet me," she said under her breath, smiling.

Near six p.m. the men ambled into the kitchen, as if some silent cue for dinner had been given. The pot roast smelled delicious as she took it out of the oven. Apache came near, looking over her shoulder as she spooned the tender potatoes, carrots, celery and onions into another bowl.

"Damn, that smells good!"

She felt her hopes rise. Gil sauntered in and drew out a chair for her. The gesture didn't go unnoticed, but no one was saying anything. Tonight the fire fighters were interested in getting their fair share of the food.

Afterward she served chocolate cake and freshly brewed coffee. Apache's eyes fairly danced with satisfaction as he leaned back in his chair, patting his stomach.

"Man, that was outstanding."

Duke shot a black look in his direction. "Anything's better than your cooking," he growled.

Leah's stomach began to knot and she lowered her gaze, feeling the tension returning once again.

"You're like a damn garbage dump, Saxon," Apache reported. "I don't think you taste the food you gulp down."

Wilson snickered. "That's why he's growing

a pot belly. If you didn't like the cookin', Duke, why'd you make such a pig of yourself?''

''Aw, cram it,'' he growled as he got to his feet, his chair scraping noisily against the linoleum floor.

''Duke, didn't you have the next lowest card?'' Gil asked.

''Yeah.''

''You get to clean up, then.''

Belligerently, Saxon placed his hands on his hips. ''I ain't cleaning up after any woman.''

Gil met his angry gaze coolly. ''You will this one,'' he answered.

Apache grinned, slapping Saxon on the shoulder as he walked toward the television. ''What's the matter, gotta eat humble pie?''

Gil rose. ''You can help him too, Apache.''

The Italian turned, a startled look on his face. ''Aw, come on, dammit, I was only teasing!''

''Fine, put your money where your mouth is, then,'' Gil ordered.

Leah excused herself, unable to take the bickering any longer. She forced herself to maintain an unreadable expression as she disappeared up to the quiet of the second floor.

Sitting dejectedly on the edge of her assigned bunk, she exhaled a loud sigh, staring down at the highly polished wooden floor. There wasn't anything she could do that would end up permanently mending the broken peace. On one hand she was indebted to Gil for his fairness in the situation. But on the other, his staunch defense of her was only going to fan the flames of dissension. She couldn't win and it was placing Gil in a difficult position with Saxon. She got up and paced the length of the room, unable to contain the feeling of helplessness within her.

If she had been a man, no one would have raised an eyebrow, much less a stink. Her green eyes darkened with pain and confusion. Was the gulf between sexes too great to bridge? She recognized that Gil was doing all he could to help her. But she worried that the situation would create a rift between Gil and his fire fighters. Might they all lash out at Gil, making the pressure on him so great that he would quit? She had seen one of her instructors down at the academy unmercifully teased because he took her under his wing and defended her. Time, she told herself desperately, time would heal the wounds that she had ripped into the fabric of the department simply by being there.

Leah was anxious to leave the station the next morning. The floors had been swept and mopped, the engines polished, and all the gear cleaned. It had been a busy night. They were called out twice, once for a smoke investigation, and the other time for a car fire. Chief Anders finally dismissed them.

"Don't forget," Gil reminded all of them, "we'll be off duty for the picnic that's scheduled for August 28th. Have your wives bring a casserole or a dessert."

"How about some of my spaghetti and meatballs?" Apache piped up, grinning broadly.

"Let your wife do the cooking," Wilson begged, raising his hand in farewell.

Leah slipped out the side door and walked to her car. It was already warming up even though it was only eight in the morning. Hearing someone come up behind her, she turned. It was Gil.

"Is the offer still good?" he called, slowing up as he approached her.

She tilted her head, mystified. "On what?"

He ran his strong fingers through his dark hair. "Either you're sending me a message to forget it or you've got your mind on something else," he commented.

She stared up at him, lips parted as she searched her mind for what he was referring to. "Oh!" she gasped. Touching her brow she murmured, "I'm sorry, Gil...no...it's the latter. I've just got a lot on my mind. I'd love to have you over for dinner soon."

He broke into a teasing smile, his blue eyes brimming with deviltry. "Name the day and time and I'll bring the wine."

"How about tomorrow evening, say seven?"

"Sounds good." He reached out and gripped her shoulder. "Get some sleep, you've got rings under your eyes. I'll see you soon."

A sense of happy expectation swirled around her as she gave the apartment one last critical survey. The last of the boxes had been unpacked over a month ago and everything was finally put away. The living room was comfortable, graced with pale yellow walls and heavy white drapes at the picture window. Two Boston ferns hung at strategic points, giving the place a look of freshness. She folded the orange and beige afghan one more time and hung it on the back of the rust-colored sofa.

While preparing the meal of seafood Newburg and the pastry shells that went along with it, Leah tried to sort out her emotional reactions to Gil Gerard. Every time she thought of his coming over for dinner, her pulse beat more strongly. She felt fear and a strange sense of elation at the same time. What did he want from her? A stolen moment in bed? An affair? He liked her, that was obvious. And it was equally obvious that she liked him...but where would it take them?

She stirred the seafood into the smooth sherry sauce and added a squeeze of fresh lemon. Despite her worries, she was determined to have a good time tonight. A knock at the front door interrupted her thoughts. She picked up a towel and walked through the living room. Gil stood there, looking in through the screen door, a bottle of wine tucked under one arm.

''Just in time,'' she said, opening the screen. ''Come on in.''

"Anyone ever tell you how beautiful you look in green?" he asked, handing her the chilled white wine. He gave her a slow appraising glance. His eyes met her curious gaze. "What did you do to your hair?"

Leah blushed slightly and turned back to the kitchen. "I put it up. I think I'm going to have to cut it because of that one place where I burned off such a huge strand of it."

Gil groaned, resting lazily against the sink. "Give me a break, Leah!"

She smiled, stirring the contents of the pan. "I know, you love long hair, right?"

Gil nodded his head. "I'd consider it a personal loss if you cut your hair."

"Mmm, would you stop flattering me? Erect that strong, silent male facade to punish me?" she teased.

She felt him come up behind her and she stiffened. His hands rested lightly on her shoulders and her heart began to pound strongly. Suddenly all the teasing banter fled and she was wildly aware of his powerful maleness as never before. He leaned down, his mouth near her ear. "I was wondering what it took to settle you down,'' he whispered huskily. ''You're too smart for your own good, lady. You have all the witty answers and great retorts to keep a man from finding the real Leah Stevenson.''

Leah trembled inwardly. His voice was a roughened whisper that evoked powerful reactions from her body. She felt his fingers slide down her arms and she drew in a deep, unsteady breath. His caress...God, it was so sure, so...experienced. Delicious shocks traveled through her at his touch and she felt him pulling her back against his hard, masculine body.

''I've been thinking a lot about you,'' he admitted. ''How you successfully evade me.''

She swallowed hard, a pulse leaping at the base of her slender throat. ''It hasn't been on purpose,'' she said, her voice sounding breathless and far away.

''No, I didn't take it as a personal insult.'' He forced her to turn around as he took the wooden spoon from her hand and placed it on the stove. His eyes were dark and turbulent as he cupped her face within his callused, strong fingers. ''Whether you like it or not, I'm going to find the real you beneath all those defense mechanisms, you understand?''

Her dark lashes swept downward and she closed her eyes, unable to deal with the ache growing within her body. Her heart was beating like a frightened bird in her chest and she suddenly opened her eyes, trying to break contact with his mesmerizing gaze. "No..." she protested softly, "don't..."

His hands moved up to her shoulders. "Don't be frightened," he murmured, searching her face minutely. He gave her a small shake. "I'm just serving warning that after working with you for two months I want a fair chance to know the real you, Leah. Not the embattled, beleaguered woman fighting to carve a niche in a male-dominated career." His hands slid from her shoulders but she remained painfully close to him, unable to say anything. He must have sensed how shaken she was because he moved away and began searching in the drawers until he found a corkscrew to open the wine.

Uncertain how to react, she grabbed up the spoon and resumed stirring the seafood mixture. Gil poured them each a glass of wine and handed one to her.

"Let's drink to exploration," he said, clinking his glass against her own. His eyes seemed to probe hers.

"No. To moderation."

He gave her a slight smile, his generous mouth curving upward. "All right, moderate exploration," he amended and took a sip.

Leah watched him warily as she took a sip of the light, dry wine. Completely unhinged by the sudden intimacy of his gaze, she took another huge gulp. No man had ever penetrated her defense systems as easily as he had just done. That made him all the more dangerous to her.

Gil put the wine in the refrigerator and resumed the conversation, trying to lighten her mood. "You are coming to the picnic on Sunday, aren't you?"

"I—haven't decided yet."

"It would be a real gaffe if you didn't show up, you know."

Anger tinged her voice. "Yes, and if I go all I'll get are stares from the wives and ugly comments from Duke. Do you think I find that comfortable to deal with?"

Gil watched her closely. "No one would. But

everyone is bringing a date or a spouse to the picnic. You don't have to go alone."

She gave him a tight smile. "That's just fine. I only moved here two months ago and I don't know anyone."

"You know me."

Her eyes widened. "I thought I did. All of a sudden you go from humorous, teasing Gil Gerard to—to..."

"What?"

She pulled out the warmed pastry shells and quickly filled them with the seafood Newburg. "Who knows what," she admitted in an exasperated tone.

He laughed quietly. "Well, at least I'm not getting cute little comebacks from you. I'll settle for your being undecided."

Leah glared up at him as she placed the main course on the table. When she came back she put both hands on her hips, fearlessly meeting his blue eyes. "I hope for your sake you aren't doing this just for the fun of it, Gil. I've had men take me on because I was a challenge to them. Some men like a strong woman. Only they like the challenge of making her submit and then they get up and walk away. Do you know how much that hurts when it happens?'' she demanded, her voice rising in anger. ''I fell for that game twice and I promised myself never again.''

''So you think I'm one of them?'' he asked, compressing his mouth.

''I don't know!'' she fumed.

He took her arm and led her back to the table. ''Come on, our meal will get cold if we stand around shouting at each other. You've worked too long and hard on this food to waste it.''

He brought over the wine and pulled out the chair for her. Leah sat down, raging inwardly. The whole evening was turning out wrong! She looked over at Gil, who was enjoying the food with obvious relish. Was she overreacting? She forced herself to eat, but she didn't really taste anything.

After the meal they sat in the living room with their coffee, Leah on the couch and he in the overstuffed chair opposite her. Some of her anger had abated, but she was still upset. Cautiously, she looked up and realized he was watching her again with that same intense gaze.

"Since you're a lady who likes new challenges, let's do something unique with our evening," he suggested easily, rising. "It's only seven and it won't get dark until nine-thirty. Let's go riding for an hour."

Leah's eyes widened. "At your farm?"

He smiled, holding out his hand. "Are you up to the challenge of it?"

She hesitated, completely taken off guard. "Well—"

"Come on," he urged. "If I leave now you'll just sit here and brood over my various blunders. I'd like to put that smile back in your eyes before the night's over with. How about it?"

How could she say no when he put it that way? She found herself liking his method of apologizing. "I'm not a very good rider—"

"I'll show you the basics. Better change clothes, though. A workday blouse and jeans would be more in order."

Five

She found herself curious about his life-style. Since their initial conversation months ago, she had wanted to know more about him on a personal level. Up until now, the appropriate opportunity hadn't arisen. "You said you lived in the city before, Gil. Do you miss it at all?"

He shook his head. "No." He gave her a sidelong glance. "These last three years since Jenny's death, I've explored some alternative ways of living."

"And you're a country boy at heart?"

He grinned. "I don't want to bore you with my life history but—"

"Somehow," Leah pointed out dryly, "I don't think your life history would be boring in any shape or form. Try me."

"Born and raised in Ohio. Actually I lived in Dayton up until three years ago when I hired on with Baybridge as a fire fighter."

"And what did you do before becoming a paid fireman?"

"Worked mostly in the construction field. I have a degree in business management from Ohio State and I dallied around with it for a number of years."

"But you were never really satisfied?" she prodded, unable to visualize him doing anything else but fire fighting.

"No, not really. I didn't find it challenging enough. I had belonged to a volunteer fire department for a long time, and I felt it was time to put up or shut up, so I went to night school and got an associate degree in fire science." He glanced at her, smiling. "The rest is history."

She leaned back against the seat, lips pursed in thought. "So you gained your insight about people from studying psychology."

"Some of it. Mostly from field experience," he assured her.

"Well, you've handled my coming into the department beautifully so far. I cringe every time one of those guys gives you a hard time, though," she admitted ruefully.

"Like I told you before, Leah, I'll back you to the hilt. You do a good job and I see no reason to leave you high and dry so they can pick you apart. I saw that happen down at the volunteer department I was at, and I swore if I were ever in a position to stop it from happening again, I would."

"What do you mean?" she asked, frowning.

"We had a woman volunteer at our station. Lucy lasted one year and then quit."

"Why?"

"The gossip, lack of support from the men. They treated her like she wasn't there, just a ghost. I give her credit, she hung in there a long time, but eventually she couldn't take it. It was a real shame because Lucy was a great fire fighter. Not just good, but great. Damn, she had good instincts out at a fire scene. I really hated to see her leave but I didn't blame her."

"I know how she feels."

"Someday, maybe all that will change."

He pulled the truck into a long dirt driveway. A two-story white farmhouse surrounded by elms and maples was visible in the distance. Leah saw two beautiful-looking horses standing contentedly near the barn as Gil pulled up to the house. He put the truck in the garage and shut it off. "Well, welcome to my humble home."

She looked around, stunned by the beauty of the farm. "It's lovely," she breathed, "and so calm and peaceful out here."

She hadn't realized how much she would feel the peace. After saddling the two horses and helping her to mount, Gil took her through a field of clover toward a stand of birch, oak, and ash. Just the pleasant *clip-clop* of the hoofs against the dry ground, the singing of the birds above them, and his presence lulled her into a state of complete relaxation. He rode at her side, their legs occasionally touching when the path narrowed. The grove gave way to another field and they rode along the edge of it.

"Given any further thought to that picnic?" he asked, breaking the companionable silence.

"Please, I'm trying not to think of it."

"You're welcome to come with me."

She gave him a long stare. "Can you imagine what the gossip will be if we show up at a social function together?"

Gil raised one eyebrow. "Nothing in departmental or union rules that says I can't escort a fellow fire fighter." He grew serious and reached out, claiming her hand. "I don't give a damn what anyone in that department says. I know that picnic will be tough for you and I'd like to try to act as a buffer."

A pleasurable tingle fled up her arm and she suddenly felt safe. "Why are you sticking your neck out for me, Gil? Let's not fool ourselves, we both know that if word gets back that we're seeing each other—"

"Stop worrying about the future," he soothed, squeezing her hand. "You have a bad habit of worrying too much."

"And I suppose you don't worry at all?"

"Only when trouble stares me in the face. My basic philosophy is to worry only about that which you can change. What you can't, you release. Simple as that."

She reluctantly pulled her hand free. He reined his horse to a halt and dismounted. Leah did the same. Gil came up to her, then stood motionless at her side.

"What does it take to stop you from running, Leah?" he demanded quietly.

"I've never run from a thing!" she snapped.

He gave her a tight smile. "Does my touching you make you uncomfortable?"

Averting her gaze, she mumbled, "No." She heard him sigh and she looked back up. He shifted to one leg, his hand resting on his slim hip.

"You're like that gray mare." He reached out to caress her cheek. "All you need is some gentle handling...."

She met his turbulent gaze, her heart pounding in her throat. Words were useless between them.

He reached out and gripped her shoulders firmly. "Don't fight me," he murmured, leaning down.

Leah inhaled sharply, stunned by his sudden, unexpected move. A bolt of lightning roared uncontrollably through her body as his mouth conquered her lips, parting them, demanding entrance. Her pulse leaped crazily. His fingers tightened against her tender flesh, his mouth growing more gentle and coaxing against hers. A new, delicious feeling soared through her traitorous body as his tongue stroked the inner recesses of her mouth. She melted into his awaiting arms. A small moan came from deep within her as his mouth urged her to participate, to become a willing partner in the kiss. His roughened fingers caressed her jaw, trailing down the expanse of her neck. Seconds became a sweet eternity as she returned the smoldering passion of his masterful kiss. His breath was warm and moist against her face when he finally pulled away from her.

Leah trembled violently within his arms, staring into his passion-darkened eyes. Her breath came in gasps; her heart thundered against her breast as she lost herself within his hypnotic gaze. "I want the right to know you, Leah," he whispered thickly.

She felt like so much moldable clay within his grasp. She melted at his touch. Her body cried with needs that had been long ignored. She exhaled shakily, lips parted and glistening.

He gave her a small shake. "Talk to me," he ordered softly.

Leah uttered a small cry and shut her eyes tightly. "Don't do this to me!" she cried hoarsely, trying to break his embrace.

"No, you don't."

"Please!"

Gil frowned, but maintained his grip on her waist. His nostrils flared with frustration. "Tell me why you're afraid," he demanded.

She felt trapped in every way. "I can't take it!" she whispered. "Not again... I—I still hurt too much...."

"No one is going to hurt you this time, Leah," he returned, pulling her close, his strong fingers running the length of her back. "I'm not Jack."

His male scent was intoxicating as she rested her head momentarily against his broad shoulder. Oh, God, just to be able to lean against him for these few seconds, she thought disjointedly. His strength was such a comfort to her.

"Are you afraid of starting a new relationship?" he demanded.

"Y-yes."

"I've purposely waited two months, Leah," he began heavily. "I wanted you to have the time to adjust to the fire department and your job. From the first minute I saw you, I wanted to know you better. I've watched you go back and forth between the firehouse and your apartment and nowhere else. You don't seem to have any other life—"

"I don't want anything else, don't you understand!" she flared hotly, jerking free of his grip. She stood outside his reach, trembling. "I had a lousy marriage, Gil. I just got rid of a man who hated everything that I am. This is the first time in six years that I've had a chance to be myself. I can't make a commitment to any man yet. I just don't have the emotional stamina it takes. Do you understand that?" she begged, close to tears.

His face relaxed perceptibly and he picked up the reins of his horse. "I can," he said softly. "You're a special woman, Leah, and finding your niche in life hasn't been easy." His brows drew downward in thought. "But when the time's right..."

She stood there, her heart pounding with anguish and hope. Shakily she reached up, brushing away the tears from the corners of her eyes. "You're a glutton for punishment, then," she said.

He offered her a quiet smile and put the reins around the mare's neck for her. "Let me worry about that. Come on, it's going to be dark in about half an hour and I want to get you home before curfew."

Leah mounted; as she took the reins their hands touched. She didn't draw away when his fingers closed over her own momentarily. The pain she was experiencing was washed away by that one touch. She believed that Gil would honor his promise not to pressure her. As he took his hand away she asked, "What curfew?"

He grinned. "The one you've set for yourself. You know, safe in your apartment before dark and don't get caught out past midnight or you'll turn into a pumpkin."

A smile edged her lips. "You're crazy," she murmured.

Gil laughed. "Yeah, I know it. Come on, fairy-tale princess, let's get you back to your castle."

His last words caught her attention. If she was a princess, then he was a knight in shining armor. She had had the misfortune of meeting men who had tried to take her to bed for a one-night stand. They cared nothing for her as a person and less about her sense of morality.

At the apartment he stood patiently as she unlocked the door. Leah turned to him, gazing up into his strong, gentle face. "Thanks for a wonderful evening," she said.

"Sure," he teased. "I got you angry and then made you cry. A wonderful evening. What are you, a masochist?"

His taunting was indulgent and without barbs. "Probably," she agreed. "Why else would I put myself through hell with the fire department just to fight fires?"

He fingered her silky hair, a wistful look in his eyes. "Or tolerate my blundering attempt to know you better?" He leaned over to place a kiss on her cheek. "You know what I like best about you?"

She shook her head, suddenly growing shy.

"I like the fact that no matter what the odds, you're determined to be yourself. I find that refreshing in a world where labels count more than individuality. Good night, Leah, I'll see you at work tomorrow morning."

Wrapped in a euphoria she had never experienced before, she watched him disappear down the stairs. Gil Gerard totally disarmed her in every way. Leah turned and went slowly into her quiet apartment, thinking deeply about him. He was different...she suddenly looked up, her eyes widening with a new discovery. He was different from the other men because he had already carved his own unique niche in the world! That realization gave her new hope and a wild, exhilarating feeling. He understood her struggles because he had already gone through them himself! Gil wasn't like other men. So why was she reacting to him as if he were in the same category? Suddenly she realized that she was as guilty of sexual prejudice as the fire fighters she worked with.

Sighing, she went to her bedroom to undress before taking a bath. Half an hour later she went to bed still considering her newfound insights about Gil and herself. In one way, she was joyous; in another, frightened to see him tomorrow morning. Leah recognized that she was now stepping outside the boundaries of her previous relationship with men. Well, she was unlike other women, so why shouldn't she be drawn to a man who stepped to a different drummer, disregarding which way the rest of the world marched?

Six

Leah felt the eyes of every member of the fire department following her as she walked to one of the picnic tables that had not yet been claimed. Her stomach was knotted and it was painful to try to seem nonchalant and relaxed beneath their silent scrutiny. She had nothing to be ashamed of, she told herself, and lifted her chin despite the pounding of her heart. Fearlessly, she met Chief Anders's smiling gaze. Leah nodded to her colleagues and spread the small white tablecloth she had brought over part of the table.

Afraid of the consequences for Gil, she had decided at the last moment to go to the picnic alone. Reluctantly, Gil had agreed with her logic.

Several children, all below the age of ten, stared openly, never having seen a woman fire fighter before. A few edged closer to where she stood unpacking her lunch. She smiled over at them. One child, a dark-eyed little girl, smiled shyly in return. Two older, more aggressive boys walked up.

"Hey! You the woman fireman?" one demanded, an imperious note in his voice.

"I'm the woman fire fighter," she corrected easily, continuing to spread her food on the cloth.

"My dad says you ain't," he prodded.

Leah straightened up and sat down on the bench, maintaining her smile. "Who's your dad, son?"

"Bob Wood," he answered proudly.

Leah gazed up at his young, freckled face.

How untouched he looked...unscarred by life, and full of promise. "And what's your name?"

"Scotty. My dad says I'm gonna be a fireman someday too."

"It's a wonderful career," she agreed.

Scotty tipped his head, frowning. "How come you ain't mad at me? Dad says you don't like men very much."

Leah burst into laughter. "He did? Goodness, that's news to me."

"He says you're trying to prove any woman can fight fires."

She relaxed, enjoying the boy's honesty. "I don't think just any woman could do the job, Scotty. Just like I don't think every boy can become a major-league pitcher. What do you think?"

Scotty looked impressed with her analogy, a slow grin spreading across his open, freckled features. "Hey...yeah, you might be right," he said excitedly. He took a few more steps forward, losing his initial fear of her. "You really go into the houses with air pak on just like the other firemen?" he whispered, his eyes growing large.

"Quite a few times lately. Why? Don't I look like I can handle it?" she asked good-naturedly.

Scotty suddenly became shy, unable to hold her amused gaze. "Nah...it's just that, well, you know..."

"No, I don't know, Scotty."

The youngster sighed and made a face. "I thought you were gonna be a sour old woman."

"Ohhh." Leah nodded confidentially. "I see..."

The other boy crept up to Scotty's elbow, gawking. "Your dad never said she was pretty!" he whispered into the boy's ear.

"What's this?" a voice asked from behind her.

Leah twisted around to find Gil standing there, hands resting loosely on his hips, a smile hovering around his mouth. She felt the heat of a blush rising across her neck and sweeping across her cheeks. He looked devastatingly handsome to her, the pale blue shirt he wore bringing out the intensity of his blue eyes. The jeans were molded to his lower body, accentuating his long, well-developed thighs. What fire fighter didn't have a strong pair of legs? she wondered fleetingly.

"Lieutenant Gerard!" Scotty piped up, running over to him and tugging on his arm. "She's nothing like we thought she'd be!"

Gil met her gaze. He ruffled the boy's reddish hair playfully. "I suppose you thought she was some old maid who would bite your head off, right?"

"Yeah, how'd you know?"

He grinned, tussling with the boy in a gentle wrestling match. "Well, that's the gossip I heard. Guess it isn't good to listen to others before you check things out yourself. Right?"

Scotty grinned impishly. Gil knelt down on one knee and opened his arms so that Scotty could fall against his body. "Yeah, I guess you're right. She's really pretty!"

"I think so too," Gil agreed, his blue eyes warm with amusement. "Why don't you three go test that lake water and come back and report if it's warm enough to swim in?"

Scotty yelped, grabbing his friend's hand. The little girl ran after them, trying to catch up. Gil got to his feet, dusting off his pants. "Mind if I sit down and visit for a moment? You looked a little lonely over here."

"Sure," she replied.

Gil leaned back, his arms against the table. "He's right you know," he said, tossing a glance at her.

"About what?"

"That you're beautiful."

Leah shrugged, secretly thrilled by his compliment. How long had it been since someone had told her that? Not that she expected every fire fighter to give her compliments. Normally they were a closemouthed group who did little in the way of sharing their inner feelings or thoughts with one another. "Thank you. You just made my day."

"You can make mine now."

It was her turn to eye him.

Gil smiled. "What's that look of distrust for?" he demanded.

She still didn't know quite how to handle his intimacy. "Don't you find it a little awkward to be seen with me out in front of the whole department? We talked about this before and you agreed that we shouldn't fraternize too much."

"I changed my mind," he returned, his tone devoid of the usual teasing note. Instead, there was a new seriousness in his voice and it registered immediately with Leah, making her feel uncomfortable and at the same time exhilarated.

"I just don't think it's wise."

"Stop worrying so much. I always see that little frown on your face."

She shrugged, embarrassed. "Concentration," she explained. "I'm afraid not to concentrate every moment on some aspect of my job for fear I'll make a mistake."

"With time you'll get over that."

If I'm given the time, she thought. She looked up, noticing several people staring in their direction. She compressed her lips.

"You sure you want to be seen with me?" she asked, her voice suddenly filled with tension.

He looked unperturbed. "I don't mind. Do you?"

"I don't know..."

"You could sound a little more positive about it," he said dryly.

She smiled wryly. Gil Gerard was too easy to like…too easy to… She caught herself, frowning. To what? Love, her heart whispered fiercely. Leah sat up, completely stunned. Good Lord! Love? How had that word slipped into her thoughts? She avoided his inquiring gaze, more rattled by this discovery than if she'd had to go into a burning structure to rescue someone.

"You okay?" he demanded. "You look a little pale."

"No—I'm fine. I was just thinking…" she stumbled.

"You seem to do a lot of serious thinking," he said, beginning to frown. "You're going to have to learn to be less sensitive around the guys and start acting more normally."

"It's my sensitivity that's gotten me this far," she flung back. "If I weren't sensitive to their moods, I'd be fired outright."

"You've paid a lot of your dues these last two months, Leah, and I'm trying to tell you to ease up and relax."

"Is this official advice?" she asked coolly.

"No, just a suggestion from a friend," he rejoined softly. "That's what I'd like to be for now, Leah...your friend."

"I find that hard to believe after what happened the other night."

He shrugged his broad shoulders. "We'll let time be the test of my actions, fair enough?" he asked mildly.

"I've never really been 'friends' with a man, Gil."

"Would you like to?" His blue eyes seemed to penetrate to her very soul.

She gave him a shy smile. "I don't know...."

"Is it the depth of the commitment that bothers you?"

She opened her mouth and then closed it. "Yes and no. I just came out of a lousy marriage where commitment was a string of broken promises." Her voice grew tired and she looked away, watching the children playing by the edge of the lake. "Is this your way of calling a truce between us?" she wanted to know.

Gil sank his chin into his hands. "I gave it a lot of thought the other night, Leah." He gave her a sidelong glance. "You need breathing room. I understand that, but I also want to let you know that I meant what I said about getting to know you better. I'm old enough to realize that instant attractions are usually a disaster in the long run and that a relationship built on time and exploration is infinitely more successful."

She gave a sharp derisive laugh. "I wish I had known that six years ago!"

He shared a secret smile with her. "But you do now, don't you? That's why I think friendship between us is a good place to start."

"This is new to me," she confided. "I've never had a man for a friend." And then she flashed him a silly smile. "Just a husband and a few would-be lovers."

"Then it's about time you explored a relationship that's been missing from your life."

"What do we do?"

"What we're doing now, talking. Sharing." His eyes crinkled as he watched her. "Do you find it painful?"

"No," she said softly.

"Good. I'm enjoying myself too."

She sat there next to him, relishing his closeness. Together they watched the children race around the tip of the lake brandishing cattails like swords. Now that she had been at the picnic for a while, Leah noticed that most of the families had returned to the enjoyment of the afternoon and fewer curious stares were being aimed in her direction.

"You like kids?" he asked, breaking the silence between them.

Leah leaned back against the table, drawing up one leg and wrapping her arms about it. "Love them. They're so much fun. It's like watching a flower blossom right in front of you."

"You had Scotty wrapped around your little finger."

She smiled tentatively. "Part of that was the fascination with the woman fire fighter image."

"You must have handled him well, because he's a pushy little kid when he wants to be. I've never seen him so attentive."

"You make him sound as if he's hyperactive or something."

Gil rubbed his jaw. "I think he is. I know he drives Bob's wife crazy."

"He seemed curious and I like that trait in kids."

He nodded. "That kid has more energy than ten put together, and a million questions up his sleeve. Better watch it or he'll hang around you from here on out."

"I could suffer a much worse fate, believe me," she answered.

"Ever have any of your own?" he inquired gently.

Leah chewed on her lower lip, staring fixedly at the green grass at her feet.

"Jack really didn't want any. He was too busy being a jet jockey and impressing other women with his status," she said, an underlying edge to her voice. She allowed the anger of the old hurts to surface. Children gave her a special kind of happiness and often, when she watched a mother with her baby, she wistfully dreamed of being in that situation someday. Being a fire fighter didn't preclude her becoming pregnant and then returning to the job after having a baby. She ran her fingers distractedly through her loose hair. The problem was finding a man. She stole a look at Gil and knew he would make a wonderful father.

"Then he was a fool," Gil said, catching her startled look. "Any man that would throw you away ought to have his head examined."

"It was my fault too. I married Jack because I thought I loved him. It was an infatuation that lasted about a year."

"You were probably too young and inexperienced to be able to know the difference."

"I don't know," she murmured. "I wonder if I'll ever really find the real pieces of myself. The me that I'm happy with even if others aren't. I'm so distrustful." She gave a shake of her head. "And that's stupid. You've always been fair with me and stood up for me when I needed help. You're the only one in the department who's never tried to make me feel small or worthless."

"You're searching for yourself, Leah," he returned gently. "We all go through growth stages when outer pressures force us to go inside and find out what we're really made of. You're just going through a reevaluating period."

"How do you know so much about the way I feel?"

It was his turn to shrug but she saw the pain in his eyes. "It was because of Jenny, wasn't it?" she asked gently.

He was silent, his face becoming an inscrutable mask. Leah got up, conscious of the tension within him. Stuffing her hands in her jean pockets, she murmured, "I'm sorry, Gil. I didn't mean to bring back painful memories."

Standing, he motioned toward the lake. "No need to apologize. Friends never need to say they're sorry for trying to understand each other. Grab your suit and towel. Let's go take a swim and get away from this crowd for a while."

Leah had worn her suit beneath her jeans and short-sleeved pink blouse. "Sounds great," she agreed, reaching for a towel.

The ground sloped downward toward the inviting blue lake, which was surrounded by cattails. She suddenly felt free, her stride lengthening as she walked at Gil's shoulder. When they reached the small sandy beach, Scotty and his two friends accosted them. Their shrill laughter of delight filled the air as they ran back into the water, begging Gil and Leah to come and play with them. In no time Leah had shrugged out of her clothes.

"You're going to cause a riot," Gil said, breaking into an appreciative smile as his gaze flowed across the lime green suit that clung to her slender figure.

Leah waved her hand at him, caught up in the enthusiasm of the children and his obvious delight. "I'm going to forget that those people on the hill exist. Right now all I want to do is revert back to a kid myself and have some fun."

She turned and skipped lightly into the water, gasping as it closed about her knees. It was colder then she'd first thought! The little girl came swimming up like a dog. Leah leaned down, scooping her up.

"And who's this little guppy?" she asked.

"Susie," the child giggled shyly.

"You're an awfully good swimmer, Susie," Leah whispered conspiratorially, putting the little girl back down. "Do you think you might swim with me out to that platform with the diving board on it?"

"Yay!" she exclaimed, clapping her hands.

Leah placed a kiss on her forehead. "Come on, I'll race you!"

By the time Leah had allowed Susie to win the "race" out to the floating platform, both boys had swum ahead and were waiting for them. Leah helped Susie climb up, treading water until the child was safely aboard.

Scotty yelled, "Look out, Leah!"

A strong arm slid across her waist, pulling her backward away from the platform. Leah twisted out of Gil's grasp, laughing. Her hair was plastered against her head, bringing out the natural prominence of her high cheekbones. Gasping, she caught the mischief in Gil's eyes as he lunged toward her a second time. He was too strong to outdistance but she was more nimble, diving down into the murky depths to escape his charge.

She surfaced yards away to the sound of the kids laughing and warning her again. Looking around, she didn't see him until she felt his hands capture her waist. In seconds he propelled her out of the water and she landed with a big splash a few feet away. She surfaced, laughing with all of them, and swam back to the platform. Gil helped her up and she sat there, watching as he pulled himself up beside her. She had never realized how truly beautiful his body was until that instant. The water glistened on his tightly muscled shoulders and chest. Dark hair covered his broad chest and flat stomach, disappearing beneath the waist of the swimming trunks.

Susie climbed into her arms and snuggled contentedly, her head against Leah's shoulder. Gil reached over, tousling the girl's blond hair playfully.

"This is Apache's daughter, in case you didn't know."

Susie looked over at him. "My daddy's not an Indian!" she exclaimed indignantly.

Leah smiled, hugging the girl and rocking her gently. She looked up, catching Gil's unshielded reaction, and melted beneath the tender flame she saw in his eyes.

"You'd make one hell of a mother," he murmured, brushing stray tendrils of hair from her cheek.

The rest of the afternoon was a melee down at the lakefront. It was as if every child knew that there was fun going on, and soon, to Leah's delight, the small beach was filled with youngsters that ranged in age from eighteen months old to fifteen years of age. Gradually the mothers came down to watch their children, as if sensing that Leah was less of a threat than they had first thought. Gil suggested a water battle, and soon they were carrying the young children around on their shoulders in the chest-deep water in sparring matches. Leah got dunked the most, but she took it in stride.

After three hours she retreated to the opposite end of the lake, where a small patch of open bank was surrounded by cattails. Flopping down on the grassy bank on her stomach, she tucked her hands beneath her head and closed her eyes. Soon after, Gil joined her, lying close by. The sun was warm, drying the water from her skin. She languished in a semidoze, a good kind of exhaustion filling her. She heard Gil get up at some point and then she must have fallen asleep.

She awoke slowly, aware of a strong hand

massaging her shoulders in slow lazy motions. Groaning, she turned toward him. Gil smiled down at her as he knelt by her side, rubbing in the protective lotion. "You were starting to look like a lobster."

Leah moaned, relishing his touch on her back. "It feels great," she murmured. "Don't ever stop." The pressure of his hand disappeared for a moment while he changed position. His fingers moved gently up the length of her spine, massaging the tight muscles. It was heavenly and Leah surrendered completely to his ministrations. His fingers were strong and coaxing against her yielding flesh as he worked her back, shoulders and neck free of tension. Another more disturbing sensation coursed electrically throughout her body. Each skillful touch of his hands stirred her senses. She could not recall Jack ever taking the time to do something like that for her. Yet Gil seemed to sense she needed it. His fingers glided up her spine, lightly caressed her shoulders, traveled slowly down the sides of her back. She was acutely aware that his fingers were within a mere inch of her breasts; she almost wished he would touch her....

"You're in good shape," he murmured. "I like a woman who is supple and has muscle tone."

"You can thank fire fighting for that," she murmured drowsily.

"Mmm, I never realized how beautiful your legs were. It's a shame they have to be hidden in a pair of navy blue slacks or bunker pants all the time," he teased.

Leah smiled. "You're not in such bad shape yourself."

"Compliments will get you everywhere."

She laughed softly. "You're spoiling me absolutely rotten, do you know that?"

"One of the small pleasures I allow myself. You're purring like a cat, lady."

She rolled on her side and sat up. Gil looked boyish, his face devoid of tension, his blue eyes warm with humor. Strands of his dark hair lifted in the inconstant breeze. Reaching out, she took the suntan lotion from him. "Turnaround is fair play. Lie down."

"That's an invitation I'll never decline," he said, lying on his stomach.

"You wouldn't," she noted dryly, pouring out the oil into her hands and warming it up before she applied it to his back. She rose to her knees and moved beside him, hands against his flesh. His muscles were firm and taut from continual workout. Leah reveled in the exercise, aroused by the touch, smell, and closeness of him. It was a pleasurable few minutes. She sat back, wiping the excess lotion off in the grass, and then lay down on her back.

He reached out to capture her hand. "Thanks," he murmured.

Her heart skipped a beat and she automatically returned the pressure of his fingers. His grip relaxed, his hand remaining on top of hers as they both closed their eyes and enjoyed the warmth of the sun. Leah lay there, her body reacting strongly to him. She hadn't forgotten the burning kiss that had seared her lips or the way the touch of his callused hands ignited new fires of longing deep within her. She sighed softly. One part of her hungered for his touch, another desired the friendship he had offered, and yet another hung back, terrified. She laughed at herself: that last part was called wisdom.

She must have dozed off again because when she awoke, she opened her eyes to see Gil propped above her, studying her with a raw intensity that made her pulse leap strongly at the base of her throat. Her lips parted unconsciously as he leaned over her. Breath suspended, heart pounding wildly, Leah felt a jolt of electricity flow through her body as his mouth descended demandingly against her lips. His hand moved to her slender neck, fingers against her jaw. He held her still so that he could taste the sweet depths of her mouth. Instinctively, her arm slid around the curve of his neck, fingers entwining in the dark curls at his nape. Fire, more raging and uncontrolled than any she had fought, swept through her with fierce new intensity. The sandpapery texture of his cheek against her face, the moist hotness of his breath fueled the flame ignited between them. She responded wantonly, unafraid to match his volcanic fervor.

His mouth moved against her lips, becoming more gentle and caressing. A soft moan rose in her throat as he broke contact, his face hovering only an inch from her wet, throbbing lips. Her eyes were wide, her breath coming in shallow gasps as he studied her in the intervening silence. "I want you," he breathed thickly, his voice trembling with husky vibration. "All of you, Leah. Every square inch of your lovely body." He groaned, closing his eyes, exhaling forcefully. "I've never wanted a woman more than you," he whispered, his eyes turbulent and hungry. Managing a shaky smile, he traced the line of her brow. "This is a hell of a fix."

She swallowed convulsively; her body trembled with desire. Finally, she found her voice.

"What do you mean?" she asked, her voice wispy.

He looked beyond her at the quiet lake. His profile was rugged. She noted that small lines fanned out from the corner of each of his eyes. He turned to meet her gaze, and a self-deprecating smile edged the corners of his chiseled mouth. "I offer you friendship and then take advantage of it. I didn't mean to kiss you.... God knows, I fought myself long enough. Just watching you sleep with the sun glinting in your hair pushed me over the edge," he admitted.

"I'm not sorry," she whispered huskily.

Surprise flared briefly in his cobalt eyes. "I don't want you to think I'm playing a game with you. I'm a strong man in some respects, but you've hit my weak spot." He laughed. "I just can't keep my hands off you."

Her heart was beginning to come back to a normal beat. She reached up and caressed his jaw and cheek. "I know you're not playing a game with me. You don't have to apologize. I liked it as much as you did."

He captured her hand, holding it tightly against his bare chest. "I wasn't going to apologize," he murmured, mirth returning to his eyes.

She smiled. "Awfully sure of yourself, aren't you?"

Gil laughed, sitting up and releasing her hand. "Hell of a beginning for a friendship, huh?"

"Yes," she murmured, "a hell of a beginning."

It was nearly dark when the picnic was officially over. They had rejoined the group near dinnertime and had helped the children roast marshmallows and wieners over the fire. The adults seemed to silently accept her within the fold upon their return. The fact that the children rushed up to them helped to break the ice. Scotty and Susie never left Leah's side for a moment, and she settled in to play with them during the long evening hours.

Leah had gotten over her self-consciousness by entertaining the children with stories around the fire. Gil remained close by her side with little Susie, finally tuckered out, asleep in his arms. Even Chief Anders was less growly than usual as he lounged near the fire while Leah told the last story of the evening. Apache got up and came over to take his daughter from Gil's arms. He smiled over at Leah.

"You ever babysit?" he asked her.

She shrugged. "I did when I was younger."

"Well, anytime you want to get another dose of this little one, just let me know. Angie was saying she's never seen Susie so taken with anyone before."

Gil smiled over at Leah. "Who said women fire fighters weren't special?" he teased warmly.

Apache laughed softly, hugging his daughter to his chest.

"Maybe you're right after all, Gerard. I'll see you two tomorrow morning. Good night."

A pleasant feeling enveloped her as Gil helped her repack her small picnic basket. Scotty had cried when his father came to take him from Leah's side. Bob managed a murmur of apology to her, thanking her for taking care of the boy for the day. She sighed, gazing up at Gil.

"It turned out to be a wonderful day," she said softly as she closed the lid on the basket.

He slid his arm around her shoulder. "Mmm, in more ways than one. Come on, I'll walk you to your car."

Leah leaned against his sun-warmed body, a smile of contentment hovering around her mouth as they made their way through the dusk. He put the basket in the back seat and held the door open for her.

"Still friends?" he asked.

"As long as you want," she whispered.

That enigmatic smile returned to his mouth, and his eyes became hooded and unreadable.

"Watch it, lady, or I might hold you to that," he warned softly.

Leah gazed up into his shadowed face, trembling inwardly over his roughly spoken words. The day had been a miracle on all levels for her. Especially the emotional one. "Gil..." she began tentatively, unsure of how to explain what she was feeling. "I don't want this day to end...." Her eyes darkened with uncertainty.

He brought up his hand and rested it on her shoulder, his fingers warm and strong. "I don't either," he returned huskily, "but it had to be your choice, not mine."

Leah nodded, agreeing with his logic. Earlier, he had offered his friendship. If he was to become her lover as well, it had to be at her invitation. She had never made a decision like this on the spur of the moment. If anything, Leah had always been afraid and distrustful. But as she looked into Gil's eyes, a new strength welled up inside her. It was right. She didn't know why, but she sensed that her decision had been good. "I'm afraid," she whispered.

A wry smile pulled at one corner of Gil's mouth. "So am I."

Leah's eyes widened. "You are?"

"Yes." His grip tightened momentarily. "We're both serious when it comes to commitments with another person." His voice deepened. "I've never considered you lightly here," he said, pointing to his heart. "I told you before, I want the right and the time to get to know you, Leah. All of you," he stressed gently. "Yes, I'm scared. And I'm deliriously happy. I'm many things all at once where you're concerned, lady." Humor glinted in his eyes. "I'm far from perfect, honey. I offered you friendship today and now I find myself wanting to take you to bed with me. I can't help it and I don't want to. But I want you on all levels, Leah. Mentally, emotionally, and—" he traced the length of her clean jawline "—physically."

Leah shivered at the sensual implication of his words. Her dark lashes fell against her cheeks. "I feel the same," she admitted.

Gil chuckled. "Come on then. I'll meet you over at your apartment. Who knows what will happen when two people who think the world of each other are this scared."

Leah laughed quietly with him. "Misery loves company, then."

Gil grinned. "You're hardly miserable to be around, lady, believe me," he returned fervently.

The transition from friends to lovers took place with unexpected ease. Gil helped her put the picnic basket and other articles away once they arrived at the apartment. Gil made himself comfortable on the couch, and Leah brought over two glasses of wine and handed him one. She curled up on the couch, facing him, their bodies in contact with one another. The languorous sensual tension that had existed between them all day increased as they sipped the dry white wine. Music from the stereo drifted through the apartment, soothing away any anxiety or fear.

Gil placed their emptied glasses on the coffee table and took up her hands. With ease, he lifted Leah to her feet. A tender light appeared in his eyes as he cupped her face with his large hands. His breath, slightly sweet from the wine, caught her senses as Gil pulled her toward him. Leah did not resist, but let the full weight of her willowy body rest against the hard planes of his more angular form. Closing her eyes, she lifted her lips to his descending, predatory mouth.

A jagged, heated bolt of lightning plunged downward through her as his mouth barely grazed her parted, waiting lips. The sandpapery texture of his skin raised prickles of pleasure in her. His mouth moved across her lips, stealing her breath. Instinctively, Leah slipped her arms across his broad, incredibly strong shoulders, pulling him closer to her arching, aching body.

Throwing all caution aside, Leah hungrily returned his demanding kiss. He groaned and drew away slightly. His breath was labored, eyes darkened with barely restrained desire, as he stared down at her.

"I need you, Leah," he whispered thickly. "God, I've wanted you ever since I first met you."

Breathless, she nodded. "Yes," she agreed inaudibly. "Love me, Gil," she whispered, raising her eyes to meet his burning gaze.

He swept her up into his arms, carrying her as if she were a fragile child. The darkness in the bedroom was eased by a thin slice of moon hovering in the blackness of the sky. The silvery moonglow sent slanted streams of light through the delicately wrought lace curtains. Her heart pounded in her breast like a wild bird that had been captured as Gil gently deposited her on the bed. The heat of his body was disturbing as he patiently worked loose the buttons on her blouse.

There was beauty in each shared movement. Leah delighted in being an equal partner in the satisfying ritual of undressing each other. As his shirt fell open at her urging she placed a trembling hand against the dark mat of hair on his chest. She lifted her chin and met his penetrating gaze. In his eyes she saw the hunger building, a glimmer of tenderness, and…love? She blinked, aware of the wiry hair beneath her palm, the sledgehammer beat of his heart, the tautness of the skin across the breadth of his well-muscled chest. Was it love? Her breath came in short gasps as his hands slid firmly upward, cupping her now naked breasts, teasing the nipples to budding life. It wasn't her imagination! She saw some undefinable emotion in his eyes, an emotion that made her yield to his masterful caress and eagerly reach up to meet his mouth with renewed fervency.

He whispered her name reverently, lying back on the bed and then bringing her to rest on top of him. Her body sang with pleasure as she settled against him, reveling in his sheer masculinity and her femininity. Blood pounded through her; the need to be one with him was now urgent. Her lips brushed his mouth, teasing, nipping at each corner. His fingers wrapped within the silk of her hair, Gil growled, gently forcing her onto her back. He drew her head back against the pillow until her lips parted to receive his kiss. Instead, he ran his tongue around her hardened nipples, taunting her unmercifully, coaxing her body into a frenzied state of need. As his mouth settled over one peak, he nipped it gently, feeling her arch upward against his body in response.

She moaned his name, fingers digging deeply into his heavily muscled shoulders, begging him to enter. A primitive passion surged hotly through her aching body and she willingly parted her thighs as his knee settled between them. Each goading touch of his skillfull fingers sent her closer to the edge. "Now," she rasped softly, begging him with her eyes, voice, and hands. "Please..."

Her breath stopped as his hand slid beneath her hips, lifting her upward to meet his thrust. An explosion of incredible pleasure jolted through her straining body and a cry broke from her lips. A tidal wave of joy surged through her and she joined him in a rhythm that carried her on soaring wings of fiery passion. He coaxed her beyond anything she had ever experienced, taking her on a spiraling, dizzying climb that climaxed in a volcanic release of utter pleasure. Leah collapsed against him. A tremulous smile fled across her lips as she felt him stiffen, find satiation within her and then grip her tightly to him seconds later. Weakly resting her head against the dampness of Gil's arm, she closed her eyes, physically drained and yet unutterably happy.

Gil rolled to one side, bringing Leah to him once again. He kissed her damp forehead, her cheek, and finally her pouty, parted lips. A new fierceness welled up in his heart as he held Leah. She brought out a side of him he'd thought long dead. It was a miracle, he decided. He loved her.

Seven

"What the hell is this?" boomed Anders as he swept down the stairs to the bay where the arriving and departing crews were waiting. His face was livid as he angrily surveyed the men and one woman standing at attention beside the engines. "All right," he growled, "I suppose you think it's a real cute joke, Stevenson."

Leah jerked her head to the left, meeting the chief's narrowed eyes. "Sir?"

"In the bathroom," Anders repeated heavily, scowling.

Leah gave him a confused look. ‘‘I don’t know what you’re talking about, Chief.’’

Someone down the line snickered and then all the men began to grin and laugh. Leah gave Gil an exasperated look. He shrugged.

‘‘What is it, Chief?’’ Gil asked after the initial burst of giggles had died away.

Anders glared at his men. ‘‘I should have known...’’ he said, and then snapped, ‘‘The next man who pulls that kind of crap is gonna find himself doing duty cleaning up clogged ditches within the city limits. Got that? Dismissed!’’

Completely perplexed, Leah took the stair steps two at a time. The two male crews mixed jovially down in the bay after Anders had disappeared. When she walked into the bathroom she stopped, gasping. There, suspended on a clothesline that had been ingeniously installed, hung a white bra that appeared to be a size 42-D cup. She tried to suppress her smile, but suddenly she broke into gales of laughter, her clear voice carrying through the bunk room. Footsteps echoing in the hall made her stop and she turned, wiping tears from her eyes. Gil appeared and he too halted, staring at the bra. A slow grin spread across his mouth and he began to laugh. Leah shook her head and went up on tiptoe to bring the bra down.

She held it out in front of her, grinning. "It's a little big, don't you think?"

"Slightly. Must be the guys' wishful thinking," Gil chuckled.

Leah colored and went over to her locker, stuffing it in the top compartment and locking it. "I wonder if it belongs to one of the guys in the off-going crew?"

"Don't be so sure it was one of them," Gil warned.

"You mean one of our guys came in early to rig this thing up?"

"Who knows?"

She managed a grin. "I think it's kind of funny myself."

"So do I. Come on, let's get downstairs. We've got some work to do."

The morning passed quickly and Leah noted that Gil's crew seemed positively happy. Well, maybe that was what it took for her to be accepted: the picnic, a practical joke, and her own ability to laugh at herself. She had seen Anders twice and each time he nodded in her direction. It looked as if things were finally going to gel and she silently thanked whoever had arranged the voluminous bra fiasco.

At midmorning they all met in the kitchen to draw cards to see who would fix lunch and dinner. Leah groaned when she drew low card. "Okay," she griped, smiling, "who's fixing these cards? This is the fifth time in a row I've had kitchen duty since I fixed that pot roast!"

Apache grinned slyly and cast a look over at Gil. "Ain't me. You keep this up and we're all gonna get fat. My wife is complaining that I'm growing a potbelly just like Duke here."

Saxon sneered, ignoring the happy banter as he continued to drink his coffee. "I ain't got no complaints from my women. They all like my body."

Leah colored fiercely, always embarrassed by his crude remarks. He did it deliberately, she was sure.

"Well, what will it be, guys?" She looked at each of them and they all hung back. "How about some okra, Sam?" she teased.

Wilson groaned. "Give me a break!" It was a well-known fact that he couldn't stand the vegetable.

Gil smiled over at her as he went to the sink and poured himself another cup of coffee. It was an intimate smile, telling her that she was handling the men well. It bolstered her confidence more than anything else could have, and she decided to give them a taste of the real Leah Stevenson.

"Well, I could make spaghetti and meatballs with a ton of garlic in it," she hinted, watching Apache's eyes light up.

"Hey! That's a great—" he piped up.

"Forget it," Saxon droned.

"How about something different? A vegetarian meal?" she suggested.

"Do we look like rabbits?" Sam shot back. And the entire crew groaned collectively, giving her a beseeching look.

"How about that good Yankee pot roast?" Gil asked.

"You've had it three times in a row! You know, since I'm a woman, my repertoire of recipes covers more than one kind of meal."

Apache howled, slapping his knee. "Hey! That's a good one."

"Just as long as it's got plenty of potatoes, I'll eat it," Saxon said, throwing her a look of warning.

Leah ignored his dark scowl. "It's about time you guys got a little more cosmopolitan in the taste-bud department. Whether you like it or not, I'm going to make beef Stroganoff tonight for dinner."

That got a smile from all the men. Even Apache knew what it was, to her surprise. She puttered in the kitchen, making sure all the spices and other ingredients she needed were there. Pretty soon the men got busy with their individual assignments and the kitchen emptied. She happily made a cake, wanting to please them. This was a special day for everyone, and the change in the men's attitudes infused the atmosphere at the firehouse with new buoyancy.

Around eleven, Gil came into the kitchen for his second cup of coffee. He looked over her shoulder as she stirred the cake ingredients furiously in the bowl. Smiling, he wiped a smudge of flour off her cheek.

"Anyone ever tell you how nice you look in the kitchen?"

She glanced at him. "Watch it or I'll get flour on you, too," she warned.

He sipped his coffee, leaning against the draining board and watching her with interest. "I didn't mean it as a chauvinistic remark. Your cheeks are flushed and the hair around your temples has curled from the sweat you've worked up by beating that poor mix to death."

She grinned as she poured the batter into an oblong pan. After wiping her hands on the poor tattered excuse of an apron she wore, she placed the cake in the oven. "Just watch what you say or I'm liable to give you no dessert, fella." She poured herself a cup of coffee and sat down at the table. Gil joined her.

"Dessert comes in many forms," he replied enigmatically. "Watching you is dessert, lady."

The sudden huskiness of his voice sent a delicious wave of pleasure through her. "And I still think you've got a degree in blarney, Lieutenant Gerard."

"Just so you don't think last night was blarney," he murmured seriously.

She blushed, shaking her head. Making sure that no one could hear them, she said, "Let's not talk about that here." Then, in a louder tone, she added, "I don't know what happened today, Gil, but they're sure acting differently toward me."

"I think it was a combination of the picnic and your cooking," he conceded.

She raised her eyes upward. "Oh, God, don't say that! I've worked so long and hard to prove myself and acceptance still boils down to pleasing their stomachs and getting along with children? I think I'll go slit my wrists!"

He smiled. "I told you time would take care of it, didn't I? But I have to admit, everyone's humor has improved since you started cooking for us."

Her eyes narrowed. "Then I was right, you are stacking that damn deck of cards."

He rose, shrugging his broad shoulders. "Me?" he asked innocently.

Leah uttered an expletive under her breath. "Now you are going to get it for sure, Gil Gerard."

"You'll personally give it to me?"

She met his glittering eyes. ‘‘In spades, fella. In spades,’’ she promised, unable to suppress a smile.

‘‘Just name the time and place, I’ll be there.’’

‘‘It isn’t what you think it is,’’ she warned, trying to maintain her threatening posture.

He appraised her slowly, his eyes lingering on her tall slender body. ‘‘Don’t bet on it,’’ he whispered. ‘‘Remember what happened last night.’’ With that he put the empty cup on the draining board and sauntered out, a self-satisfied look on his handsome features. Leah laughed softly, recalling all too well the ecstasy they had shared.

They had no more than finished their lunch when the fire alarm droned through the bay.

‘‘Dammit!’’ Apache howled, leaping off his chair.

‘‘They plan this!’’ Sam swore, scraping his chair back and rising.

Leah compressed her lips. Adrenaline was shooting through her.

STRUCTURE FIRE AT 55 NORTH BRADFIELD, the dispatcher announced.

They all ran for their gear simultaneously.

Sam jerked on his turn-out coat as he ran for Lady. A moment later he was starting the engine. She roared to life, filling the bay with the deep growl of the diesel engine, echoing off the walls.

"Leah and Apache," Gil directed, "air pak."

Leah gave him a stare as she trotted past him. It was the first time he had ever allowed her to be on the first team in a major structure fire. Her blood pumped strongly as she sprang up on the running board and threw herself into the jump seat. Apache leaped into the seat across from her, still muttering.

"Dammit, I ate too much. I hope I don't throw up. Damn! I don't wanna lose this lunch." He glanced up at her. "Hell of a lunch, Leah."

The engine revved up; lights whirled and the siren started to wail as they pulled out into the blinding sunlight. When Leah had tightened her shoulder straps, she looked up at Apache. "Thanks," she called.

She tried to talk herself out of her nervousness. First team! God, she couldn't let Gil or Apache down! She ran over the air pak procedure, testing the equipment twice to make sure everything was in good working order. The engine swung heavily around street corners, its air horn blasting several times when motorists wouldn't yield to the truck. Anxiously, Leah searched for the telltale smoke. As they headed out of the major part of the city toward the middle-class suburbs, she saw gray-and-black columns hanging a hundred feet above the trees in the distance. Her mind raced with possibilities: were there kids home? A mother? How about a senile older person who couldn't walk or was bedridden? The smoke would kill them within minutes if they were trapped. She began to recite a familiar litany over and over again: Please God, don't let there be any children in there. Adults had the presence of mind, the strength, and the larger lung capacity to withstand smoke, heat and a crisis much better than a child. A child, she knew, frequently froze or hid. Either way, the child could die because of improper fire training by his parents. Leah twisted her gloved hands together in her lap, aware of the tenseness that always inhabited her before they arrived at the scene. Once there, she would relax. It was the not knowing that made her so anxious.

When they arrived Saxon wrapped the hydrant, which was a good two hundred yards from the two-story house. Leah jumped off the engine and quickly assessed the house. Smoke was leaking out beneath the eaves, which meant heavy heat buildup. She searched for people....

"Grab that two and a half and take it up to the front door," Gil ordered Apache.

A frightened young girl of fourteen was screaming near the front door. Several other people ran up. An older woman grabbed Gil's arm.

"There's a kid in there!"

"How many?" he asked, his voice suddenly devoid of emotion.

"The mother's at work. She leaves the two of them with her," the woman cried, pointing at the babysitter. "Oh, Lordy..."

Leah bit back a cry and looked toward the house. They had to hurry! Oh, God, no...no...

Her heart began to pound unevenly and it seemed as if everything was a mass of confusion around her. The girl and the woman were screaming at Gil and then Gil was ordering an ambulance and calling in a second alarm. She and Apache dragged the two and a half up to the door, approaching it cautiously. In the distance more sirens wailed mournfully in the humid noon heat. Leah was taking larger gulps of oxygen from her air pak. They approached the door and knelt down by it. Apache gingerly twisted the knob. The door flew open; smoke spewed out in large ugly clouds. He motioned to her.

"Let's go!"

Gil ran up to them, gripped Apache's shoulder, and leaned over. "Go to the right. The babysitter says the two kids were asleep in the last room to the right," he shouted.

Suddenly the charged hose seemed light to Leah as she helped haul it into the darkness of the house. The heat was intense; the skin on the back of her neck was smarting. Leah could hear the roaring of the flames somewhere to their left, the creaking of burning timbers, and a heavy, dropping sound. Simultaneously, she was aware of windows being broken to ventilate the house. More shouts could be heard in the cottony darkness as they groped their way forward into the last room on the right.

Apache found the first bed. He grabbed Leah's coat frantically. "Here!" he cried, his voice muffled by the mask he wore. "Take the kid. Find a window. Get him out!"

She didn't know if the inert form was a boy or girl. Cradling the small child against her body, she crawled on one hand and her knees around the end of the bed. Using her outstretched hand, she blindly followed the wall until she found a windowsill. There was no time to try to find a latch. She laid the child down at her knees and fumbled for the spanner wrench she always carried in her pocket. Finding it, Leah protected the child from the shattering glass as she smashed out the window with the wrench. Instantly she heard another fire fighter's voice. Forcing herself up on her knees, she leaned out the smoky window yelling, "I've got one of them! Take him!"

She handed the unconscious child through the window and then got back down on all fours, crawling along the wall, trying to find her partner. Sweat stung her eyes and she gasped deeply. Saliva trickled from the corners of her mouth as she searched the gray blackness for Apache.

"Apache!" she cried, stopping. Where was he! Damn, he should have remained with her! Never lose contact with a team member. He could be in trouble and she would never know it. "Apache!" she screamed until her voice cracked from the strain. Doggedly, she followed the wall, praying she would run into the second bed. He would be there, she thought desperately, trying to find the second child. She yelled again and again. A new sense of dread overwhelmed Leah, and she crawled faster, keeping one hand stretched outward, hoping to come into contact with furniture or a body.

She ran into him full force. Grabbing him she cried, "Apache?"

"Yeah, yeah. I got the other one. Where the hell's the window?"

She hesitated, sobbing for breath. In smoke, disorientation was commonplace and she had been trained to follow walls and not rely on her memory. "This way," she called. "Grab my ankle."

Apache grabbed the leg of her bunker pants and they made their way back around the wall. The MSA bell on her air pak started ringing wildly, alerting her that she had only three minutes of air left. Her pulse skyrocketed and she frantically tried to hurry, but it was impossible because Apache was dragging the child with him. Leah tried to limit herself to taking half breaths. It was damn near impossible under the circumstances and she desperately hugged the wall, trying to locate the window. The MSA Apache was wearing began to ring too. The sound of the bells clamored terrifyingly in the smoke.

It was an eternity before she found the window. Without thinking, Leah shoved Apache and the child ahead of her. Suddenly, her air was gone and she sucked deeply, trying to breathe. Blindly, she helped to lift the child up. Closing her eyes, she forced herself to remain calm, to loosen the emergency bypass valve on the regulator so that she could get the last vestiges of oxygen. She felt Apache get up and then he was gone, having escaped to safety through the window. Blackness tinged her vision as she rose up on her knees. Oxygen starved, she fumbled, her gloved fingers splayed outward, reaching for the window. Wildly, she clawed at the suffocating air mask.

Strong hands gripped her by the shoulders and Leah was dragged forcefully through the broken window. She landed hard, hitting the ground and then rolling over on her back, clawing at her mask. Darkness closed in on her and panic consumed her. She had no strength left to even unscrew the hose from the regulator. Voices...men yelling...someone jerking at her air pak harness...it all melded together. Suddenly fresh air flowed up into the mask and she panted, taking shallow, ragged breaths. Her eyes fluttered open. Too weak to move, she was vaguely aware of someone loosening the straps of the air mask, pulling it off her face. The sunlight made her squint and she rolled over on her side, gagging. She lay crumpled in a fetal position like a rag doll, vomiting. She was only aware that someone remained at her side, his hand protectively resting on her shoulder.

Got to stop hyperventilating, she thought dazedly, utterly spent. She heard Saxon's strained voice yelling over the cacophony sounds. The man above her answered and she realized it was Gil. Leah continued to gasp, eyes tightly shut.

"Leah?" he called, bending over her, his eyes dark with worry. "Babe, are you all right?"

She shook her head. Her lungs ached, her stomach roiled and knotted threateningly. "Air," she whispered hoarsely.

More noises. Ambulances, fire engine sirens, the pumps screaming like shrill banshees, the cry of men under stress. She heard Gil ordering a resuscitator. Leah sobbed for breath, aware of his hand on her shoulder. It seemed only seconds before he pulled her over onto her back and placed a plastic face piece over her mouth and nose.

"Breathe deep," Gil ordered, "it's pure oxygen."

She did as she was instructed and was surprised at how quickly her head began to clear. Within a few minutes he had her sitting up while she took deep breaths of the life-giving air. She looked up to see ladders leaning against the second-story window. Fire fighters wearing air paks and carrying hoses were coming down from it. The smoke was dissipating. She saw Apache lying prostrate nearby, his face haggard and streaked with gray, greasy smoke. A paramedic ran up and knelt at his side, giving him oxygen to help revive him more quickly.

Gil rose to his full height, watching her worriedly. "I've got to help the chief, Leah. Stay here until I tell you to move."

You won't get any arguments out of me, she thought wearily. Her attention was drawn to the ambulance and it took several minutes before her mind would function properly. The children! Without thinking, she staggered drunkenly to her feet and moved toward the two units. She was oblivious to the fact that she was still wearing her air pak. All she cared about was finding out the condition of the children. As she drew near the ambulances, she heard a woman crying hysterically and someone else shouting at her.

Three paramedics were working over a small red-haired child of three or so and another of about six. The mother, no older than twenty-five, was screaming, her fingers digging into her skull as she watched in horror. Leah swallowed against rising bile, her gaze riveted to the children. It wasn't fair! Anger more chilling and frustrating than anything she could ever express rose up in her. They couldn't die! She and Apache had rescued them...they should live. God wouldn't let them die!

The paramedics were grim faced, their words limited to terse orders for other instruments or equipment. The IVs were being suspended above the children, making the whole scene look grotesque and surrealistic. The mother continued to hover hysterically over the men working with her children. She grabbed at one paramedic's arm and he jerked away, anger clearly written in his expression. The woman was momentarily taken aback and turned, her eyes wild as she spotted Leah standing nearby.

The mother's mouth stretched into an ugly snarl and she lunged at Leah, fists clenched. "You should've been here sooner!" she screamed, striking out senselessly.

Stunned, Leah felt the first blow land against her shoulder.

"It's your fault! Your fault!" the woman sobbed, beating at her wildly.

Leah broke out of her shocked stupor and raised her arm to protect herself. She stood at least five inches taller than the mother. A thousand confused thoughts roared through her head as she tried to grab the woman's flailing arms. Under the turn-out gear, her face blackened by smoke, Leah knew she was not recognizable as a woman.

"Stop it!" Leah commanded, grabbing one of the woman's hands and jerking it downward.

The woman sobbed, striking out again, this time with far less force.

Tears blinded Leah's vision and she made a desperate lunge for the other hand, capturing it. The mother suddenly stopped fighting, her body buckling. If it hadn't been for Leah, she might have injured herself by striking the hard asphalt surface. Instead, Leah broke her fall. She knelt down, allowing the mother to lean wearily against her body. The woman was sobbing without restraint, gripping Leah's black coat, her knuckles white and bleeding.

"I'm sorry," Leah choked, holding the

woman. Distractedly, Leah ran her gloved hand against the woman's short dark hair. "We tried, we tried so hard.... We don't want your children to die. God, we want them to live," she whispered brokenly.

"My babies...my babies..." the woman cried hoarsely, clinging to Leah.

Leah shut her eyes tightly, resting her head against the woman, fighting back a sob. "I know...I know..." She held the woman in a viselike grip as the efforts of the paramedics intensified. Their voices were charged with a high degree of emotion, something that rarely occurred. But children were involved and that snapped even the most controlled professional's composure. It had already broken Leah's. Dully, she listened to the battle being waged for the second child's life.

It seemed like hours before the paramedics brought the boy back, but finally they got a response from him. Slowly, Leah got to her feet, pulling the mother up with her. Leah walked her over to the second ambulance. The woman needed to be tranquilized or given some sort of sedative. Leah helped her up into the cab.

"Look, I'm going to get someone to help you. Just sit here. Will you do that for me?"

The mother's face was ashen, devoid of any emotion now. Shock had set in and she barely acknowledged Leah's request.

"I'll be right back," Leah promised, her voice thick with unshed tears. She trudged wearily back to the other ambulance, finding one of the paramedics standing above the youngest boy.

"Do you have a second?" she asked.

"Yeah. What is it?" he wanted to know wearily, watching the red-haired boy on the gurney.

"The mother...she needs something. I think she's going into shock," Leah explained.

"Okay. Thanks for getting her off my back. I couldn't have worked on that second boy if you hadn't got her attention."

"Sure." Her voice sounded hollow to her ears and she wiped away a trickle of sweat running down her temple. "Just try to help her."

"We'll take care of her."

"Will—will the second boy make it?"

"Dunno. He stopped breathing once from smoke inhalation. It could happen again at any time...."

"What about the other one?"

"He'll be okay."

Leah turned away, fighting back the anguish that was threatening to rob her of all control.

He patted her shoulder. "Glad you were here. We owe you one."

Leah blindly stumbled away and nearly ran into Gil. He gripped her arm, his face suffused with anger.

"Where the hell have you been?"

She looked up dully, her blackened features streaked by tears. "Here, with the mother," she answered, her voice a whisper.

His fingers tightened. "Dammit, when I tell you to stay put, you stay put! You understand me?" His eyes were angry thunderclouds. "I was worried sick. I thought you'd crawled off somewhere and were more seriously hurt than I'd first believed!"

His snarling voice only added to her pain. "I—I'm going to be sick." She turned away before leaning over and retching again. Bile stung her mouth and tears flowed down her cheeks. She heard him curse and felt him release the hold he had on her arm. Sinking to her knees, she was wracked by dry heaves until she thought her stomach would destroy itself. Moments later Gil was back with a paramedic.

He leaned down and helped her to stand. This time there was no anger in his voice. "Come on, you're going over to the hospital."

"No..." she cried softly.

"No argument. Apache is already on his way there, so you'll have company. Come on, babe...."

Eight

Leah lay morosely in the emergency room, smelling of smoke and exhaustion. They had stripped her out of the sweat-soaked turn-out gear. The doctor had checked her lungs, given her an antispasmodic for the vomiting and decided to keep her there for observation. She was too distraught and physically incapacitated to care about the strange looks she had received when they wheeled her in on the gurney. Apache had looked no happier. Exhausted and suffering from smoke inhalation, he was lying in another makeshift room across the hall. She lay there, eyes closed, unable to sleep, unable to forget....

When she awoke she had no idea how long Gil had been standing there watching her. A doctor calling sharply to a nurse to assist him with a cardiac case had startled her awake. Gil reached out, smoothing back damp strands of hair from her forehead.

"How do you feel?" he asked.

"Like hell," she answered thickly.

"It was a bad fire."

Tears swam in her eyes and she blinked several times. Leah searched his grave, exhausted features. "Will the kids make it?"

He managed a broken smile, continuing to caress her face tenderly. "Both of them are in good condition now. You and Apache are the ones we're concerned about."

"I feel okay."

"You don't lie very well, babe."

"I may look like hell but that doesn't mean I can't go back to work," she protested, her voice raspy.

"You aren't going anywhere."

Leah groaned. ‘‘What will the guys think if I can’t go back to work, Gil? I’ve got to go—’’ She made an effort to sit up. He placed his hand on her shoulder and firmly pushed her back down.

‘‘The guys think you did one hell of a job under the circumstances,’’ he said, scowling at her. ‘‘Apache said you didn’t have to give up your place at the window.’’ He tapped her shoulder and his voice took on a warning note. ‘‘Next time your air pak bell starts ringing first, you leave first. Don’t play Mary Martyr and die from oxygen starvation like you damn near did today.’’

Anger flared in her green eyes as she stared up at him. ‘‘I had to save the children,’’ she spit.

His entire body tensed. ‘‘Yeah, and you could have ended up on a morgue slab,’’ he snarled. He gripped her arm, giving her a small shake. ‘‘Dammit, I won’t lose you, Leah. Not this way. What you pulled today was stupid. How in the hell can we possibly rescue others if we throw our fire fighters’ lives away during a crisis? What if there had been other people in that house and we were shorthanded? You would have had to go back in and get them, too. Even more people could have lost their lives because you were being heroic. In this business you learn to live to fight fire another day. You learn to think on your feet when people are going to pieces around you. God, if we don't, then everything will be lost. Don't you realize that?''

Her heart was pounding with anger and anguish. She jerked free of his grip, breathing heavily. ''Get out of here,'' she gritted through her teeth. Tears filled her eyes as she thought of the children who had almost died. Suddenly her anger evaporated and she rolled on her side, her back toward him. ''Just leave me alone,'' she sobbed, gripping the pillow against her face.

''I'll be back in a little while,'' he answered, his voice cold with fury.

Leah was no longer cognizant of time as she rode back to the station in the fire chief's car along with Apache and Gil. They were ordered by Chief Anders to pick up their civilian gear and take the rest of the day off. Fire fighters from another crew would take their places for the duration of their shift.

Apache was withdrawn as Gil drove them home. Leah remained silent, riding in the front with Gil. More than once he glanced at her, but said nothing. When they dropped Apache off at his house, Leah saw the fear etched in his wife's eyes as she came out to the split-rail fence to meet her husband. She embraced him for a long, touching moment.

"I'm okay, Angie," he mumbled self-consciously, raising his hand in farewell to them.

Leah couldn't stand the look of love and concern on Angie's contorted features. Leah looked down at her tightly knotted hands, compressing her lips, glad to be on her way home. The icy silence in the station wagon grew and she shrank inward.

At the apartment building he parked the car and shut off the engine. Gil turned and appraised her.

"You sure you'll be all right?" he asked, concern in his husky voice.

She refused to meet his eyes. Jerking up her purse, she opened the door and started to slide out of the seat. Almost immediately she felt his hand on her arm. Gil's fingers stung like a white-hot brand and she strained against his tightening hold.

"At least you can be civil and answer my question," he said, his tone maddeningly calm.

Leah jerked around, her nostrils flared with fury. "Don't worry, Lieutenant, I'll be around another day to fight another fire for you. That's all you care about—another trained body to fight fires, right?"

His mouth compressed into a thin line and he gave her a measuring stare. "You know I care about you."

She broke his grip and perched on the edge of the seat, breathing hard.

"I don't believe a damn word of it," she said quietly. "At the hospital you were all business. Just a cold and unfeeling machine spewing official rules."

His azure eyes became stormy as he stared at her. "What are you implying?" he whispered, his voice dangerously low.

"You were only interested in enforcing regulations, Lieutenant. It was obvious you didn't really care about those children or—" she swallowed hard, her last words choked out "—or about my feelings!" She heard him snarl something but didn't remain long enough to hear it. She got out of the car and hastily slammed the door behind her. Taking the steps two at a time, she walked quickly to her apartment, digging distractedly in her purse for the keys.

She heard his footsteps and turned, key in hand. Her heart plummeted as Gil gripped her and spun her around to face him. His face was contorted, eyes burning coals. "Don't you ever run away from me again when you say things like that," he warned.

"I'm off duty," she hurled back, wrenching herself free and jamming the key into the door. She twisted the knob and threw the door open.

"But still responsible for your words and actions."

"I won't apologize for a thing I said!" she cried. "I think it's sick to put anyone or anything before a child's life. You'll never get me to change my mind on that. Now just get out of here and leave me alone!"

He stood over her, his nostrils dilated with fury as he glared down at her. As tears streamed down her dirty cheeks, he winced visibly.

"Dammit," he whispered harshly, gripping her by the shoulders, "you don't understand, do you?"

He was so close, so overpoweringly strong. And she felt so utterly exhausted. Leah placed her hands on his arms, trying to steady herself. "Understand what?" she cried, a sob in her voice.

Suddenly the implacable hardness in his face dissolved. "I nearly lost you out there today," he rasped. His grip tightened until she felt pain race up her arms. "I won't lose you, Leah...I won't."

Confused, her vision blurred by her own tears, she searched his taut features. What was he saying? His voice was quivering with feeling, with...suddenly she surrendered to the violent emotions of the last few hours. A soft sob rose in her throat.

"Oh, honey," he said raggedly, pulling her to him, stroking her hair. "God, how I love you." The words were forced out by the knowledge that she could have very easily died in that fire. Gil had seen other fire fighters die because they'd run out of oxygen in smoke-filled structures. But Leah was alive. And he loved her with a fierceness that overrode his normal logic. He rocked her gently back and forth in his arms, crooning words of comfort in her ear. Finally she stopped crying.

"Come on," he urged, "you need a quick shower and bed, in that order. You're exhausted, Leah."

Numbly, she allowed him to guide her to the bathroom. Her mind felt like a vacuum. He brought in her robe as she painstakingly unbuttoned her blouse with trembling fingers. "Leah?" he questioned softly at the door.

Lifting her chin, she stared across the small space that separated them. Her lips parted, wet with spent tears. Her heart contracted with unspoken love for Gil as she saw the worry in his storm-colored eyes. "I'll be all right," she assured him.

Nodding, he closed the door.

The hot shower cleansed away the sweat and smoke from her skin. She emerged much later, the maroon robe wrapped tightly around her body. Her hair hung in dark, damp sheets about her shoulders because she didn't have the strength to dry it properly. Gil appeared at the end of the hall. She halted a few feet from him, having trouble forming a coherent sentence. "I need sleep...."

"I know," he murmured, placing his arm around her shoulders. "Come on."

Wordlessly, Leah allowed him to guide her to the bedroom. He threw back the covers and ordered her into the bed, making sure she was properly tucked in. Her eyelids felt as if they were weighted with lead.

Gil leaned over, caressing her hair. "Go to sleep, honey."

Those were the last words she remembered as she sank into the chaotic, emotional abyss of sleep.

Her sleep was punctuated by reoccurring nightmares of the house fire. She felt herself suffocating within the confines of the face mask, clawing wildly at the regulator. Swirling smoke surged around her and Leah heard herself screaming for help. She jerked upright in the bed, sobbing, holding her throat. Her eyes were wide with fear, her breathing irregular and convulsive. It was still daylight, though the rays of the sun were slanting low through the window.

Gil opened the door and walked quickly to her side. Leah lifted her head, an imploring look written on her taut features. Without a word he sat down and gathered her into his embrace.

Just the strength of his arms eased the trauma of the nightmare. "Shh, it's okay," he soothed. "You're just having a bad dream, honey."

Shutting her eyes tightly, Leah slid her arms around his waist and buried her head against his shoulder, seeking the safety he offered. The heavy, steady beat of his heart sounded like a soothing drum in his broad chest. She was aware of his hand stroking her silken hair, of his fingers gradually trailing down her shoulder and then moving in small circles meant to relax her. Bits and pieces of reality began to filter into Leah's sleep-drugged mind. She became aware that Gil smelled fresh, as though he had just showered. Somewhere outside the apartment window, a bird sang melodically. Her breathing quieted and she felt herself responding to the touch of his hand upon her back.

She had almost died today. The thought struck Leah full force for the first time. Her fingers tightened against his back. Another thought struck her: she remembered Gil close to tears earlier, telling her that he loved her. Leah nuzzled his neck and jaw.

Lifting her head, she stared into his dark, concerned eyes. He cradled her face between his callused hands, tilting it upward to meet his descending mouth. This time she did not pull away. This time Leah reached out, eagerly meeting his strong mouth. The fierceness of his masterful kiss took her breath away.

"I love you," he whispered raggedly, kissing each corner of her responsive lips. "You're mine, you always have been." His mouth pressed against hers more insistently, forcing her lips to open, allowing entrance of his tongue into the honeyed depths of her.

A moan of pleasure vibrated in her throat and she pressed shamelessly against him, her breasts growing taut, the nipples like hard pebbles against the wall of his chest. Drugged by his kiss she broke away, her voice husky. "Love me, just love me...."

His mouth closed upon hers in hungry abandonment, creating a fire storm of longing deep within her body. She had slept in the robe, and her body was naked beneath its folds. The sash was pulled away and she held her breath, waiting, waiting for his hand to touch her trembling body. Her lips parted with anticipation as he slipped his hands beneath the folds of the cloth, his fingers moving up her rib cage toward the fullness of her ripe, straining breasts. A cry of longing bubbled up into her throat as he caressed her, his fingers brushing the hardened nipple tentatively. Her fingers sank deeply into his shoulders when he lowered his head, his searching mouth finding the nipple. Fire shot through her lower body as his mouth moved temptingly upon her breast. He nuzzled first one and then the other, until she felt a scream of need for him building into an uncontrollable frenzy of hunger.

The robe fell away and she felt the cool air

on her heated flesh. It seemed only moments before he had stripped the clothes off his magnificent body. Gil moved her over, lying down beside her to complete what he had started. She searched his impassioned blue eyes, knowing with unbridled joy that she loved him just as fiercely as he loved her. Reaching up, she slid her arms around his massive, corded neck and pulled him down upon her. A groan escaped him as he placed his arm beneath her hips, forcing her against him, making her fully aware of his arousal.

She arched joyously, her body a perfect fit against his own. He kissed her eyes, nose, mouth, and trailed a series of nipping kisses down the length of her slender neck. She held her breath, anticipating his torturous mouth upon her nipples. Within seconds, his mouth closed over the first one, robbing her of all thought. She slid her hand down his lean torso, across the hard flatness of his stomach, and caressed his thigh and hip. He stiffened against her as she teased him.

''God, Leah,'' he groaned thickly against her ear, his breath hot and moist.

She pressed the length of her body against him. "Now, please now," she begged breathlessly. "I need you, I love you...." Then once again she was transported into that world of incredible pleasure he had introduced her to. His fingers trailed down the expanse of her belly and hip, lightly teasing first one thigh and then another. A hungry ache throbbed in her lower body as he gently parted her legs, his hand stroking the sensitive flesh of her inner thigh. She quivered as he caressed her body. A whimper of need rose in her and she felt his knee settle between her legs. Blindly she arched her hips, ready to receive him, needing him. A cry of pleasure reverberated within her as he thrust deeply into her.

He brought her into rhythm with himself, moving her through heights only they two could reach together. She gripped him, a white-hot explosion erupting within her, leaving her breathless and spent against his rock-hard body. Mindlessly she lay within his arms, completely satiated. Seconds later she heard him groan; his body strained against hers. She reveled joyously in his release, clinging to him, whispering soft words of love against his damp face.

Gil gently took her into his arms afterward and covered them both with a sheet. Leah lay pressed against his length, aware of their hearts thundering against each other. She rested languidly on his chest, the silken hair tickling her nose. She felt his hand settle on her head and stroke her hair. Tears rolled down her cheeks as she allowed the avalanche of emotion she felt for him overtake her. He touched her face. Finding wetness, he rose up on one arm, placing her protectively beneath his body. He regarded her gravely.

"Tears?" he demanded huskily. "Did I hurt you, honey?"

She closed her eyes, loving his concern. "No...no, it was wonderful. You were wonderful. We were wonderful."

She felt him chuckle and he leaned down, kissing each eyelid in turn. "Tears of happiness, then?"

Opening her eyes, she drank in the sight of his strong, handsome face. She had never seen Gil look so relaxed. Dark strands of hair lay damply against his brow and she reached up to brush them back into place. "Yes, I'm very happy," she admitted softly.

Gil caught her hand and pressed a lingering kiss on her palm. He became more serious. "A good part of my reaction at the fire was because I loved you, Leah. I thought you knew that. That was why I was so upset when you left the scene and went over to help the paramedics."

Her throat constricted with tears. "No—I didn't. I—oh, I don't know what I thought," she admitted. "I've never worked a fire where children were involved, Gil. It shook me up more than I realized. When you started yelling at me, I couldn't understand it. I was so torn up emotionally. I wanted those kids to make it."

He caressed her cheek absently, staring across the room in thought. Finally he gazed down at her. "I damn near lost it when Saxon yelled and told me he'd heard your air pak bells go off. The smoke was so bad that we couldn't get near the windows unless we had air paks on ourselves. Didn't you hear us screaming at you?"

She shook her head. "No…I had just found Apache and was in the process of trying to get him and the other child out."

"Well," he said grimly, "I sent in a rescue team with extra air bottles to try and find you."

Her eyes widened. "You did?"

"Yes. About the same time Apache produced the second boy at the window. Saxon yelled that he didn't hear your bells anymore so we knew you were going down for the count. Things got pretty tense then."

Leah shivered within the warmth of his arms, recalling all too vividly the entire scene. "I felt Apache go, so I knew there were fire fighters there at the window," she said. "I was blacking out even before I reached the sill. I don't remember much after that." Her voice trailed off and she gave Gil a guilty look. Her heart wrenched when she saw the anguish in his face. Leah slid her fingers along the damp curls on his massive chest. "I'm sorry, Gil. I didn't mean to make you worry. I had a one-track mind at that point."

He pressed her hand against his chest. "Smoke was roiling out that opening and I kept low, thrusting my arm inside the window to try and find you. Apache managed to tell us that you were right behind him. If necessary, I would have climbed in after you."

Leah realized the foolhardiness of that action. A fire fighter without proper oxygen equipment was as good as dead if he tried to enter a smoke-filled building. "So you were the one who found my hand and jerked me out of there?"

"Better believe it, lady. Your face was gray and it wasn't from the smoke, either." He took a deep breath. "God, Leah, I was never so scared. You were gray from lack of oxygen."

She managed a sliver of a smile. "I felt a little gray around the edges."

Gil picked up a strand of her hair, moving it slowly between his fingers. "Why didn't you stay where I left you, honey?"

"I had to find out about the kids." Her voice became strained. "I felt personally responsible for them, Gil. Do you understand?"

He nodded grimly. "All too well. There have been a couple of times when I went over to the hospital after we rescued children just to make sure they were okay."

Her heart turned over with love as Leah realized that he was just as deeply concerned about the children as she had been. "I owe you an apology,'' she whispered, slowly sitting up. Her hair tumbled across her shoulders in a rich cascade, covering her breasts. She drew up her knees, resting her arms against them. ''All along I thought you really didn't care, Gil. I should have known better but I was emotionally strung out.... I wasn't in full control of myself.''

He lightly caressed her arm. ''Don't apologize for that, honey. There isn't a rookie fire fighter alive that isn't on the verge of losing control the first, second, or even third time children are involved in a fire. Some fire fighters never get used to it and they take stupid risks, jeopardizing their lives as well as the victims'.'' He raised his grave eyes, meeting her gaze. ''And right now, you're in that category.''

It was true, she conceded. Leah rested her chin on her knees, deep in thought. She felt Gil sit up, felt his arm go around her and draw her back into his embrace. She didn't resist; she needed the comfort he was offering.

''Look,'' he began heavily, ''this has been a rough day. I want to take you home with me, Leah. I want to spend the next two days with you.'' His voice vibrated with emotion. ''Lady, I love you. I almost lost you. I think we deserve the time with each other. How about it?''

Leah turned, throwing her arms around his neck. ''Oh, Gil,'' she whispered against his chest, ''take me home. I—I don't want to be alone right now.''

He embraced her long and hard. Finally he released her, his gray eyes glittering with unshed tears. ''Good. Maybe, if you're up to it, we'll go visit the hospital tomorrow and see how those kids are coming along.''

Her heart exploded with love for him. Without a word she nodded, her green eyes wide and lustrous. Leaning forward, she touched his mouth with her lips. He groaned softly, then pulled her down on the bed, back into his arms. The afternoon sun slanted through the lace curtain, lending the room a golden glow. Leah settled into his embrace, completely content with his nearness.

Nine

Leah stretched languidly, awakening to the sound of pots and pans being clattered in the kitchen. Her mind was spongy with sleep as she rolled over on her back. Then she realized that she was at Gil's farmhouse. Her eyes widened slightly and she looked to her left where he had lain during the night. The sheets were cool to her touch. How long ago had he gotten up? The mouth-watering aroma of bacon frying wafted temptingly into the room.

A soft smile came to her lips and Leah threw

the covers back, then reached for her robe at the end of the bed. Despite her excellent physical condition, every muscle in her body protested. She wrapped the maroon robe around her slender body and tightened the sash.

Gil was whistling cheerfully when she entered the brightly papered kitchen. Sunlight cascaded through the curtains, spilling across the polished linoleum floor.

"Well, good morning, sleepyhead," he greeted, turning and smiling at her.

Leah had the good grace to blush as she moved over to him. "Don't even bother telling me what time it is," she murmured.

His blue eyes softened with tenderness as he looked down at her. Gently, he drew her into the fold of his arms. "God, you look beautiful," he whispered, then leaned down and caressed her lips.

A new warmth began to uncoil within her and she tasted his mouth with delicious slowness. Finally she pulled free, her green eyes sparkling. "Were you going to surprise me with breakfast in bed?" she asked.

He returned his attention to the bacon, carefully lifting out the fried strips and putting them into a paper-lined basket. "Yes. You were sleeping so well that I didn't have the heart to wake you." And then he gave her a wicked look. "I damn near did anyway. You're not easy to resist."

She poured herself a cup of coffee and sat at the kitchen table, enjoying the peace that the farmhouse and his presence provided. "At first, I couldn't sleep because of those nightmares," she confided, stirring a teaspoon of sugar into her cup.

"You were restless at first," he agreed. "Later on you settled down. One egg or two?" He held them up.

"Two. I'm starved."

A gleam came to his cobalt eyes. "You make me starved, too."

Leah grinned. "You're terribly good at hinting, aren't you?"

He gave her a wicked smile, but said nothing. He cracked the eggs, then dropped them with professional ease into the skillet.

A new feeling of happiness swept over Leah as she watched him make breakfast. Outside, a rooster crowed several times and one of the mares whinnied. Gil looked incredibly masculine in his jeans and a red polo shirt. She vividly recalled the sinewy expanse of his broad chest and his strong, tightly muscled legs. Even now his jeans molded his thighs, showing their lean, tapered length to advantage. Her body responded automatically to his male beauty. They had made love yesterday afternoon and the night before. The feelings of those precious hours still lingered in her body and in her mind. She stared at his hands, strong yet gentle.

Gil turned around, bearing the breakfast on a tray. He proudly presented her a plate filled with eggs, home fries, and toast. ''It's edible,'' he assured her, curbing a smile.

''Is there anything you aren't good at?'' she asked with a smile.

A twinkle appeared in his eyes. ''I don't know. Is there?''

His voice was low and suggestive, sending a shiver through her. Pretending to ignore his comment, she buttered the toast. ''Are you always this sure of yourself?'' she shot back primly.

Gil laughed, then reached over and touched her flushed cheek. "When I know the lady loves me, I am," he said huskily.

Her heart thudded at the sensuality in his tone. Leah closed her eyes momentarily. "Gil..." she began awkwardly, "we have to talk..."

Squeezing her shoulder, he whispered, "After breakfast and after you've gotten dressed. Hurry, or the eggs will get cold."

By nine a.m. she was dressed in a pair of apricot-colored slacks and a white short-sleeved blouse. Leah vaguely remembered packing a small overnight bag with Gil's help the evening before, but not much else. Her exhaustion had been so complete that she recalled very little. Wandering out the back screen door, she saw Gil in the paddock petting the two part-Arabian mares. Halting, she watched as he spoke in quiet tones to the attentive animals. Both mares stood near his shoulder, nuzzling him. They were content to be in his presence. Wasn't she the same way? Gil had that steadying effect on humans and animals. Memory of the traumatic fire came slashing into her reverie.

With a wave of his hand Gil motioned for her to come and join him. Leah walked at a slow pace. She approached the white-painted fence and leaned over the top rail.

"You all right?" he asked, giving one mare a final pat before slipping between the rails to join her.

"Yes and no," she admitted.

"Listen," he said, placing his arm against the post closest to her, "you'll remember this fire for a while, honey. Fire fighting is the only profession besides police work that can give you wartime nightmares and daytime flashbacks," he said grimly. "Tell me what you're feeling inside."

He put his arm around her, drawing her close. Gratefully, Leah rested her head in the hollow of his shoulder as he guided them through the small fruit orchard on the other side of the corral.

"I'm afraid," she confided. "And I don't know whether it's because I almost suffocated or because I almost wasn't able to save the children."

His mouth drew in at the corners and he nodded grimly. ''You've received a one-two shot, Leah. Not only did you run out of air, but other lives were at stake besides your own. I can remember the first time I ran out of air and how scared I was when it happened. Fortunately my partner was a seasoned veteran and he saved my life.''

She gazed up at him, unable to imagine him almost dying. Gil was so vital and strong. ''How did it happen?'' she wanted to know.

Gil stopped under the bough of an apple tree. The fragrant smell of ripening apples surrounded them like a perfume. Bees buzzed lazily through the warm morning air. ''We were trapped on the second floor of a house. I had just joined the department as a volunteer and I didn't even bother to check the gauge on my air pak to make sure I had a full supply of air in the tank. My partner, Bill, always checked his before he ever put it on.'' Gil smiled wryly, remembering that day clearly. ''I ran out of air ten minutes into the fire. When I grabbed at my hose and started panicking, Bill knew what happened. He yelled at me to hold my breath and then unscrewed the end of the hose on my tank.

He put it on his own so I could get a breath of air from his tank. God,'' he whispered fervently, ''I was never so scared. I had a hell of a time trying to keep my head. We were disoriented in the smoke, but luckily we found the stairs and made it out to safety.''

Leah shivered. ''That was too close. Down at the academy they drilled it into our heads that running out of air could make us panic.''

''They have the Situation Maze down there. That kind of training should help some,'' he offered.

Leah recalled the maze. It was a house trailer that was designed to put rookie fire fighters through a series of tests to simulate actual conditions in a burning structure. Their face masks were taped to make them ''blind.'' Like everyone else, she had crawled around on her hands and knees for nearly half an hour groping her way through a series of mazelike problems. ''Yes, and I did pretty well.''

''Did you run out of air?''

She nodded. ''Just like everybody else. I made it to the window and I felt the air going. I started to release the hose from the regulator so I could breathe but the instructor yelled at me. I spent another twenty seconds gasping and clawing to find that damn window."

Gil smiled. "Did you?"

"No. The instructor told me to release the hose. I never thought a breath of fresh air could smell so good." She frowned. "It felt even better yesterday when you pulled that mask off my face." She lifted her chin and stared deeply into his eyes. "I owe you my life."

He smiled lazily. Slowly, he brought her into his arms, hands resting on her shoulders. "There's only one way you can repay me, lady," he murmured enigmatically.

Her lips parted. "I don't understand...."

Gil raised one eyebrow, merriment in his blue eyes once again. "Think about it" was all he said.

The day had turned hot and humid by midafternoon. Thunderclouds were building up in the west, promising the possibility of rain by early evening. Leah was drying the dishes from lunch when Gil ambled back into the kitchen.

"Sure you're ready to go visit those children?"

Her green eyes darkened with the memory of their pale ashen faces. "Yes, I have to," she said, almost to herself.

He came over, drawing her near, resting his head against her hair. "Okay," he murmured, "it might be good therapy for you. Every fire fighter has to deal with his or her emotions when it comes to children."

"You don't have to come," Leah protested.

"Are you kidding? Come on, we'll take the pickup."

Her face was damp with perspiration as they entered the air-conditioned coolness of the hospital. Gil had mentioned that burn cases were airlifted by helicopter to a major burn center in Pittsburgh. But other than that, the hospital was equipped to handle all major injuries. At the desk the nurse directed them to the pediatric floor where the two children were being kept for observation.

Gil clasped her hand, giving her needed strength. Leah looked up at him gratefully. How did he know that she needed him at this moment? Her heart blossomed with even more love, if that were possible. They halted at the door. Leah recognized the mother instantly. Gil offered the woman a friendly smile as they quietly entered the room. Both boys were sleeping peacefully under their oxygen tents.

"Mrs. Barbara Griffin?" he asked softly.

The woman rose and tiptoed out of the room to join them. She wore a perplexed expression on her face as she looked first at him and then over at Leah. "Yes?"

Leah reached out to touch her arm. "We're with the fire department, Mrs. Griffin. Gil and I wanted to come by and see how your boys were doing," she explained.

Barbara Griffin's eyes widened. She was pale, with dark circles beneath each of her eyes. "They're going to be fine. Are you the ones who rescued Billy and Tad?" she asked, her voice strained.

Leah's throat constricted with sudden emotion as she saw the other woman's tears gathering in her dark brown eyes. "Well—"

"Leah and Apache rescued your boys, Mrs. Griffin," Gil interjected.

"Oh," Barbara sobbed, gripping Leah's arm. "I struck at you! I'm sorry. That was horrible of me. It's just that—"

Leah held her hand tightly. "I understand, Mrs. Griffin."

"Please, call me Barbara. Oh, God, I owe you so much. All of the fire department," she sobbed softly.

Leah traded an anguished look with Gil, who promptly put his arm around the woman, leading her to the nurse's station. The elevator doors opened and Duke Saxon and Apache walked out. Introductions were made by Gil, and Barbara gripped each one of their hands, thanking the two male fire fighters.

"What is this?" Apache demanded, grinning broadly over at Leah and Gil. "You two just had to check on the boys, didn't you?"

"I see we weren't the only ones," Leah noted.

"What are you doing back on duty?"

"Ah, my old lady was sitting there wringing her hands, smothering me with all this extra attention just because I got choked on a little smoke," Apache admitted. He grinned carelessly, his brown eyes twinkling. "Angie was pretty upset over the whole thing, but I told her I wanted to get back into the swing of things, to keep from getting jumpy about the near miss."

Leah noticed that Duke was also in the fire fighter's uniform of serge blue trousers and light blue shirt. Apache carried a portable radio on his belt in case a fire call came in.

"How are the kids?" Apache wanted to know.

"They're sleeping now," Gil explained, "and they've got normal color."

Apache clapped his hands together. "Great!" He came over to Leah and wrapped his arm around her shoulders. "You did a hell of a job, Leah."

Gil frowned. "You should have pushed her out the window first," he growled.

"Things got pretty intense in there, Lieutenant. I had to leave the wall to find the second kid and got disoriented. If Leah hadn't come back for us..." He gave Leah a wink. "Like I said, I owe you."

Barbara Griffin had dried her eyes and was listening to the easy banter between the fire fighters. She continued to wring her white handkerchief between her frail, thin fingers.

"You all seem to take this incident so lightly," she said, her voice hoarse. "How can you? You could have died, too."

Leah traded a look with Apache. The Italian fire fighter gave the biggest grin he could possibly muster. "Not with Leah as my partner, ma'am. This lady is somebody you can really trust in a tight situation. She had everything under control. And she's really the one who saved the boys. Me? I was out crawling around on my hands and knees trying to find the wall again after I located your second son."

Leah blushed beneath the compliment, thrilled to hear how Apache felt. None of the fire fighters had ever given her a direct compliment before. Finally the last of the barriers had been removed between her and the men. She was no longer looked upon as a woman fighting fires, but rather as a fellow fire fighter. Her heart swelled with elation and she blinked back tears. Even Duke Saxon grudgingly nodded his massive head. Leah noticed that the hate no longer gleamed in his eyes when he regarded her.

Suddenly the fire alarm sounded on the radio

Apache carried at his belt. They all exchanged a tense look as he picked it up and called into the station.

"This is a three-alarm signal thirteen," the dispatcher said.

Leah drew in a sharp breath. A three-alarm meant that there was a fire somewhere in the city that demanded every available fire fighter, whether on or off duty.

"Roger the signal thirteen. We're here at the hospital with Lieutenant Gerard and Leah."

"The chief is rolling now. He says to get to the station and pick up your gear."

All of them moved quickly toward the elevator. "Roger."

"Engine twenty-four will be ready to take you to the scene," the dispatcher said, signing off.

Silence dropped upon them in the elevator. Leah's heart was beginning a slow pound. Each fire fighter's face became devoid of emotion, their eyes intent, mouths set. She looked up at Gil.

"Where do you think it is?" she asked, knowing that the location of a fire was never broadcast over the air. If it were broadcast, there would be every reason to expect unnecessary gawkers at the scene, creating traffic congestion that might impede the progress of the fire engines and ambulances.

Gil lost his implacable look as he gazed down at her. His chest constricted with very real fear. Leah had not recovered physically or emotionally from the experience of yesterday's fire. She wasn't ready to work yet, but he knew she wouldn't stand by idly in the three-alarm blaze. Grimly he pursed his lips. "Probably one of the five-story apartment buildings," he admitted.

Leah's eyes widened and she gasped, "Oh, God...no!"

None of them said anything as they raced from the hospital to the fire department car. Apache slid into the driver's seat, throwing on the switch for the lights and siren as they roared out of the parking lot.

Leah clenched her fists in her lap, her mind racing ahead. Apartment building fires were notoriously dangerous. There would be adults, elderly people, and children to think about rescuing or evacuating. She broke into a cold sweat. That meant air pak again. She would have to enter smoke-filled apartments with a partner and search for people…

Gil gripped her hand. "Leah…"

"No. I'm going!"

His eyes darkened with pain. She had spoken with such force and conviction that there was no way he could talk her out of it. "It's going to be bad," he warned.

Her green eyes narrowed. "Tell me what fire isn't?"

His grip tightened on her hand. "There might be children involved," he warned, his voice barely audible.

"I can handle it," she ground out.

When they arrived at the station Leah's training took over. Everything became a blur as she went through the automatic motions of getting her gear, leaping on the pumper, and riding to the scene of the fire. As she stepped off the beavertail, Leah felt her emotions go dead. No longer was she trembling from adrenaline as she looked up at the five-story apartment building. She took in the fact that smoke was pouring out of the third-story region. A new calmness invaded her as she walked around the corner of the pumper with Apache to await Gil's instructions.

Every available piece of fire apparatus from the city as well as from three volunteer fire departments outside city limits was on the scene. A dozen white-and-yellow hoses lay like fat slugs across the lawn and parking lot. They were strung from the whining, screaming engines or from nearby hydrants, pouring thousands of gallons of water into the fire. Leah shut off her hearing to the cries, the sirens, and the crowds of gathering people. Sweat trickled down her temples. The heavily insulated turnout gear was stifling in the ninety-degree summer heat.

Gil met her solemn eyes. "You and Apache get on air pak," he ordered tightly.

This is it, she thought, moving through the motions of sliding the forty-pound air pak across her shoulders and strapping it tightly to her body. A new sense of steadiness made her feel even more sure of her capabilities. Apache had lost his smile. He gave her a nod of his head as he finished tightening the air mask over his face.

"Let's go, Leah," he yelled, gripping her arm with his gloved hand.

Gil put a restraining hand on her shoulder. "Leah," he called.

She halted, made a half turn toward him. Her heart wrenched in her breast as she saw the worry etched on his grim features. She reached out and touched his arm. "I'll be okay," she called loudly through the mask.

He took a step closer. "I love you, just remember that."

Tears scalded her eyes and she nodded at him mutely. "And I love you...."

He compressed his mouth, then gave them a nod. "Okay, get going. Apache, the chief wants you two up on the third floor. Just be damn careful."

It was seven-thirty in the evening and the temperature was hovering around eighty-two degrees. Leah sat tiredly on the curb with Apache at her side. Her face was streaked with gray smoke. Tendrils of her dark hair had escaped from beneath the helmet liner that framed her face. She was numb with exhaustion just like every other fire fighter at the scene of the seven-hour fire. Tiredly, she pulled the helmet off, freeing her hair, feeling the cooler air hit her hot, sweating skin.

"Oh, God, I never knew air could feel so divine," she whispered, allowing the helmet to rest at her side on the curb.

Apache barely gave a nod. He was resting his head against his drawn-up knees. She placed an arm around his drooping shoulders. "You okay?" she asked, her voice hoarse and raw.

"Yeah...just so damn tired I could fall over. Man, that was a hell of a fire."

She licked her dry, cracked lips. "It was. But we got everybody out. That's what counts." It was interesting that all fire fighters saw the success or failure of their efforts in terms of saving lives, not property. Leah gazed wearily at the line of pumpers, most of which were now shutting down. They had contained the fire to four apartments. And how many people had they rescued? She lost count of how many times she and Apache had shuttled back and forth down the smoky halls finding trapped people and taking them to the safety of the nearest exit stairs. Dully, all she could recall was going through one tank of air after another. The only rest they had had was the time it took to slide one tank out of the harness and to put another one in. At those times, someone would thrust a glass of water into their hands so that they wouldn't become completely dehydrated.

"Well," Apache finally muttered, "you feel like walking back to the pumper and stowing these air paks?"

She didn't want to move. She didn't know if she had the strength to stand. Her mind was occupied with only one thought: Where was Gil? Had he gone into the area of the fire or had he stayed back and acted as one of the tactical officers who directed the movements of the fire fighters? She hoped the latter. Finally she got up enough strength to answer.

"We may as well go back now, I guess. Think they'll have some water for us?"

Apache grunted and stood slowly. "I hope so. Sam's pretty good about finding some for us when we've been working a fire like this.

Come on, grab my hand.'' He put out his dirty, charcoal-smeared glove toward her.

Leah grasped it. Her knees trembled as she straightened up. The air pak hung heavily on her slack shoulders, and it felt like someone was pushing her into the ground because of it. They shuffled silently for more than a block before reaching the pumper. Leah was always amazed at the number of policemen and onlookers who milled around. The fire scene had become something akin to a carnival. She was too tired to even be angry about it; instead she searched for Gil.

Sam greeted them as they trudged wearily up to the rear of the pumper. ''You look bushed,'' he observed, helping them both out of their air paks.

''Just a little,'' Leah said, unsnapping her turn-out coat and shrugging out of it. Mournfully she looked down at her clothes, the same blouse and slacks she had put on that morning: they were ruined. Her hair was plastered against her skull, wet from the monumental physical exertion she had demanded from her body. ''Where's Gil?'' she asked Sam.

"Gil? He's up on the third floor with the chief checking out the extent of the fire damage."

"Did he stay down here most of the time?"

"No. The chief ordered him into the fire to direct it. The chief coordinated everybody else out here."

Her green eyes widened with silent alarm. Apache turned his head to the left, studying her. "He's okay, Leah." A grin pulled at his mustached mouth. "You kinda like the guy, don't you?"

She looked forlornly toward the apartment building in the distance. "Just sort of," she returned softly, no longer caring if anyone knew of their love for each other.

"I got that hint when Gil grabbed you before we left to go up on the third floor. I thought he was going to cry."

She wearily rubbed her face, feeling the grit upon it. "He was worried that I wouldn't be able to stand the physical demands because of the fire we fought yesterday," she explained. Fighting two huge fires back to back always made the situation more dangerous for a fire fighter.

Apache got up, stretching his wiry body in slow motion. His brown eyes danced with amusement. "You think I'm some kinda of dunce, Stevenson? Don't you think I know love when I see it?" He hit her shoulder lightly with his fist. "I'm your partner, remember? Partners know each other pretty well. So cut the bit about you being tired from yesterday."

Her teeth were white against her dirt-streaked face when she grinned. "What do you want? A confession?"

Sam interrupted, bringing them paper cups filled with water. They eagerly consumed four cups each before satisfying their thirst. "You two just sit here and rest," Sam ordered. "There's not much to do until Gil and the chief get back."

Apache leaned back against the truck, closing his eyes. "So when's the big day, Leah?"

"What?"

He opened one eye and looked at her. "Remember, I'm your partner."

She smiled wearily, running her fingers through her bedraggled hair. "He hasn't asked me, Apache," she admitted.

He crossed his arms against his chest and grinned confidently. ‘‘He will.’’

They sat there another half hour before Gil returned. Leah rose to her feet as soon as she saw him break free of the crowd. His yellow turn-out gear was dirtied and smeared with black stains. Leah anxiously perused his features, aware that he was just as exhausted as they were. He was also in air pak and she started forward, realizing his shoulders were slumped with tiredness. A hundred questions whirled in her mind but she was intent on only one thing: reaching his side to help him off with the gear.

Gil offered her a broken smile as she approached. In one hand he carried a portable radio that he had used throughout the fire to direct the various fire fighting teams. In the other he had his helmet, which dangled in his fingers by the leather chin strap. His blue eyes lighted up with pleasure as he met her worried gaze. Despite her exhaustion she looked beautiful. The white blouse she wore clung to her like a second skin. The wide red suspenders which held the black bunker pants up around her small waist looked out of place against the white material. Ordinarily he wouldn't have displayed any kind of affection toward her in public. But it had been a hell of a fire and he had worried about her throughout the hours of the holocaust. Shoving the portable radio into his coat pocket, he reached out with his right arm and pulled her up against him.

Leah uttered a small cry and threw her arms around his neck, holding him tightly. "Oh, Gil," she sobbed, "I was so worried about you."

He laughed quietly. "Worried about me? God I was worried about you, lady."

Tears streaked down her cheeks, making white paths through the grime. She drew away and gazed up into his strong, handsome face. "I was fine," she choked out, her voice growing hoarse. "We got a lot of people out, Gil. I love working with Apache. It's as if we read each other's minds."

He swept her back into the fold of his arm, relishing her closeness, the pliant curve of her body against him. "And I love you," he whispered fiercely. "Come on, we've got to wrap up and then we can go home," he murmured in her ear.

The clock struck nine inside the quiet farmhouse. The horizon was pale pink as the last light of the long day faded from the sky. Leah followed Gil through the house toward the bedroom. They had opted to get cleaned up at home instead of at the station. Technically, they still had the next day off. Turning on a light here and there, he led her through the bedroom and into the large bathroom.

"First things first," he murmured, resting his arms lightly across her shoulders. "Let's take a shower, eat, and then hit the sack."

It sounded wonderful. Gil urged her to get cleaned up while he found some leftovers in the refrigerator to make a dinner for them. The hot, pummeling stream of water wiped the layers of sweat and grime off her body. It also relaxed all her sore, tired muscles so that by the time she emerged from the bathroom, she could barely keep her eyes open. Gil met her at the kitchen entrance and guided her to the table.

"Here, sit down," he coaxed. He put a plate

filled with a rich beef stew before her. "Eat," he ordered. "I'll take my shower now. When you get done, get into bed."

Leah nodded, grateful for his attention. She watched him as he walked through the kitchen and disappeared into the living room. His shoulders seemed so wide that it looked as if he wouldn't make it through the entrance. Shaking her head, she realized her mind was so muddled that she wasn't seeing anything straight. She picked up the fork and forced herself to eat even though her appetite was nonexistent.

Gil had just come out of the bathroom in his light blue terry-cloth robe when she entered the bedroom. His dark hair lay plastered against his skull, gleaming wetly in the weak lamplight. There were shadows of exhaustion beneath his eyes.

Leah threw back the covers on the bed. "I don't know who looks worse," she muttered, "you or me."

Gil grinned tiredly, draping the towel over one shoulder and running his strong fingers expertly through his hair to tame the strands into place. He came around the end of the bed, reaching out and pulling her into his arms. The terry-cloth robe was coarse against her cheek and smelled freshly laundered. She inhaled the scent of him, sliding her arms around his large torso to give him a long embrace.

"I love you," she whispered. She closed her eyes, content to rest against his seemingly tireless body.

Gil leaned down, placing a kiss upon her hair. "I think you're sort of special too, lady," he murmured. He held her at arm's length, his blue eyes dark and hungry with simmering desire. "I just have one question for you before we keel over."

She tilted her head, her green eyes wide and lustrous with love. He was so warm, so vibrant. A soft smile curved her pink lips. "What?" she asked huskily.

Gil looked at her and then the bed. "You know, I sort of like having you around here." He caressed her cheek fondly. "I don't want to come home to the farm after putting in twenty-four hours at the station and be alone."

Her heart filled with joy as she stared up at

him. Her lips parted but words wouldn't come. She saw him smile, his azure eyes warm with love. "But—"

"Say you'll stay here with me forever," he ordered quietly, cradling her face between his large hands. "Say you'll be mine forever, Leah."

Tears gathered in her eyes and her lips trembled. "Yes," she whispered. "I've wanted to be with you since the first day we met."

Gil groaned softly and crushed her to him. They stood there for long minutes in one another's embrace. Finally he released her, his face revealing his happiness. "Listen, we've got to sleep," he said. "I was going to ask you to marry me today before the fire." A rueful smile pulled at his mouth. "I couldn't sleep now if I didn't know your answer. You're important to me, honey. More important than anything else."

She laughed throatily, burying her head against his shoulder. "But right now, we both need sleep desperately." She reached up and kissed his strong, responsive mouth. She melted in his embrace as he ardently returned her impulsive kiss. A soft moan rose in her throat; a coil of fire moved quickly up through her body. His tongue tantalized her, tortured her with a sweet promise of fulfillment. She sagged heavily against him, her breath coming in uneven gasps. Finally he broke free of her, his blue eyes burning.

"Sleep first," he growled in her ear. He placed a series of small nipping kisses down the length of her slender neck. A delightful shiver of urgency coursed through her. "When we wake, you aren't going to be safe," he promised thickly, guiding her to the bed.

Leah snuggled close to Gil, her body fitting perfectly against his, her arm and leg thrown casually across him. She closed her eyes, content with his nearness. So much had happened in the last thirty-six hours. She had made love to Gil. Two major fires had occurred. And each time, lives had been saved and nearly lost. And best of all, Gil wanted her for his wife...his partner for life. A small sigh escaped her as she burrowed against his shoulder. Her dark hair lay like a blanket across his massive chest, his hand cupping her face in the silken tangle.

Despite overwhelming exhaustion, her mind struggled briefly with problems that would still have to be faced. With the fire fighters' acceptance of her as one of the team, her job would be easier and the pressure to perform would be less. Would the chief force her and Gil to work different shifts? How many husband and wife fire fighting teams were there? Leah slid her fingers across the wiry hair of his chest, unable to answer all her questions. It didn't matter. It would all work out because she and Gil had the maturity to make the compromises that were necessary. Their love for each other would overcome any barriers.

With that thought, she gave in to the fingers of exhaustion that pulled her downward into slumber. When she awoke in the morning it would be the first day of their life together. Half-asleep, she felt Gil shift position and bring her closer. His warm, moist breath lightly fanned across her cheek. There was a wonderful reassurance in his nearness. He had been close to her since the first day they had met, and now that closeness had blossomed into the miracle of love. Love that was born too near the fire, but had risen like the mythical Phoenix to bring them glowing new life.

* * * * *